The Ventara Adventures
The Resilience of Hope

Merry Christmus
2024
XOXO

Taillyn

Merry Christmas
2024
xoxo

The Ventara Adventures
The Resilience of Hope

Hans David Müller

First Edition

Wet Ink Books
www.WetInkBooks.com
WetInkBooks@gmail.com

The Ventara Adventures: The Resilience of Hope
by Hans David Müller

Editor–in–Chief: Richard M. Grove
Editor: Miguel Ángel Olivé Iglesias
Art Director: Richard M. Grove
Chief AI Literary Prompter: Richard M. Grove
Chief AI Art Prompter: Richard M. Grove

Typeset in Calibri
Printed and bound in Canada
Distributed in USA by Ingram,
        – to set up an account – 1-800-937-0152

Library and Archives Canada Cataloguing in Publication

Title: The resilience of hope : the Ventara adventures / Hans David Müller.
Other titles: Ventara adventures : the resilience of hope
Names: Müller, Hans David, author. |
Grove, Richard M. (Richard Marvin), 1953- editor
Identifiers: Canadiana 20240496698 | ISBN 9781998324132 (softcover)
Subjects: LCGFT: Science fiction. | LCGFT: Novels.
Classification: LCC PS8626.U44138 R47 2024 | DDC 813/.6—dc23

Dedicated to
my wife
Christina
and my
trio of kids,
oh and my cat.

Table of Contents

Viktor Frankl – "In the darkest times, seek meaning; hope will guide you through."

Paulo Freire – "Hope is an act of defiance; it fuels the struggle for freedom."

Søren Kierkegaard – "Faith is a leap into the unknown, sustained by the hope that meaning exists."

An Introduction
by the Editor,
Miguel Ángel Olivé Iglesias

Dear Readers,

The endless strife between good and evil comes again under Canadian writer Hans Müller´s adventure-seeking pen. This time, the author gives us a far scenario, as far as that far, far, far away galaxy we all know about through the film *Star Wars*, an all-time favourite of Müller´s. When we read *The Ventara Adventures: The Resilience of Hope*, we perceive *the Star Wars* forces at work that George Lucas bequeathed to us. Science fiction is an old theme/genre; however, we are always enraptured by the futuristic scenarios and tricky intrigues it proposes.

The Ventara Adventures does not let us down. Müller manages to blend descriptions of rampant technology and heavy-armed conflicts with an underlying romantic touch that accompanies characters and depictions of settings. As I said, the novel limns idyllic realities in contrast with the havoc wrought by an imperialistic mind. The author uses poetic, metaphorical language that delivers a wondrous, utopian portrayal of Radiant City, the capital of the Lumina Sector:

> *"In the heart of the city lies the Grand Park, an oasis of green amidst the urban landscape. Here, ancient trees spread their canopies wide, providing cool shade to picnickers and joggers alike. The park's centrepiece is a pristine lake, its surface sparkling under the midday sun (…) rowboats glide leisurely across the water (…) Surrounding the lake, meticulously maintained gardens burst with colour, their blooms a testament to the Lumina Sector's commitment to the idea that beauty is interlocked with harmony and harmony promotes beauty."*

Such images clash against the ominous arrival of the enemy forces. As readers, we are thrust into a maelstrom of utter trepidation:

> *"Suddenly, the peace is disrupted by the distant roar of engines. Massive starships, dark and foreboding, cast long shadows*

over the city, their sleek, menacing designs a stark contrast to the vibrant life below. The once-clear skies are now filled with the ominous silhouettes of these enormous vessels, blocking out the sun and casting a pall over the cheerful cityscape."

In reference to the characters, analyzing their evolution in the main story, and backstories the writer flashes back to in their dialogues or reminiscences, we can better understand their motivations, relationships, and ultimately, their impact on the plot. The lead character, Kael Ventura, despite his decision to retire and go live in a remote location, is shocked by the news reaching him about Princess Quann´s capture.

The majority of readers will coincide that one of the key characteristics of science fiction is the creation of fantastic worlds brimming with state-of-the-art technology, strange creatures, and wars of an epic magnitude. A richly imagined universe unfurls, sparking fantasy in the readers, who will tend to take sides, most of the times, with the invaded and the weakest. This is quickly presented in the novel: Muller´s resourcefulness allows him to synthetically introduce characters, context, plot thickening, and what menacingly looms over Radiant City and the galaxy:

> *"It is the year 2165. With the approaching ships the galaxy teeters on the brink of intergalactic war. The malevolent Chancellor Virox, driven by his insatiable thirst for power, orchestrates a ruthless operation to capture Princess Quann of the Lumina Sector."*

No matter how distant we are from 2165, we cannot help but hear bells ringing when we read about a conspiracy that echoes so many on-Earth similar ones. Thus, there is evident symbolism in the novel, not just because of the author's ability to weave a rapidly moving narrative that resembles earthly occurrences, but also because events and characters revolve around inner battles of *resilience* and *hope*. In these two elements lies the ultimate symbolism in the story: a staunch adherence to hope buttressed by the power of resilience to confront and overcome seemingly insurmountable obstacles. This is how the writer puts it:

> *"With the galaxy plunged into chaos as Chancellor Virox's dark plans came to*

fruition. Princess Quann's capture was a devastating blow to the forces of good, but her defiant spirit remained unbroken. As the call for a hero echoed across the stars, the stage was set for Kael Ventara to rise to the challenge. Despite his desire for peace of mind, the call to rescue Princess Quann drew him back into the fray... Embarking on a daring mission to rescue the princess, Kael would once again become a beacon of hope in the epic saga of bravery, rebellion, and the timeless struggle between good and evil."

This is not an exclusive domain of the characters in the novel. The extraordinary philosophy of hope and resilience has been man's anchor for survival in the most adverse of circumstances. The author constantly reminds us of that in the characters' lines or his own account of facts. Symbolism is a powerful literary device that can add levels of meaning to a story. There are both animate (people) and inanimate (Kael's starship) figures in *The Ventara Adventures* representing symbols like bravery, faith, confidence, resolution, gratefulness, friendship, support, bulwark, refuge and so on. By exploring these symbols, we can uncover between-the-lines connotations and discernments of the characters and their motives.

Another aspect that stands out in the novel is the author's knack to knit emotions of all sorts in the characters. Protagonists and antagonists embody classic hero/villain features. None will hide their emotions, either personal or social, and will voice them in their dialogues or we will read them in the writer's words. It is true they are stereotypes the public is familiar with, but Müller gives us sentient characters, who love, believe, suffer, react, unfalteringly face their destinies and engage in life-risking skirmishes and missions to save other people dear to them. Therein we find some of the essential messages and accomplishments of the novel.

These characters are placed within situations that are vital in establishing the leitmotifs I have referred to: hope, determination and valor. They play a major role in infusing import to these significant values. These values mirror their formative backgrounds and are built not in isolation but in group relations, which reflect other related virtues like friendship, solidarity, trust, etc. As well, they operate on the conviction that a better future is possible. Through acts of kindness, sacrifice, perseverance and <u>mutual help</u>, characters demonstrate the power of hope in overcoming danger and harsh times. Group work, teamwork and unification are fundamental in moments of hardship, and the characters know that:

> *"Nearby, Kael sat on another cot, being treated for a wound on his side. 'We're going to need everyone's help. The Federation, the rebels, anyone willing to stand against Virox.'"*

As individuals who unite to fight evil, they are symbols their followers admire and will be willing to join or defend at all costs. We see that in Princess Quann:

> *"… her fierce determination, her unwavering spirit in the face of adversity. Princess Quann was more than just a symbol of hope for the Lumina Sector; she embodied the resilience and strength that represented the Galactic Federation. Her leadership was a beacon, guiding them through the darkest times. She inspired loyalty and courage, qualities that made her not just a leader, but someone worth fighting for."*

Determination is another basic theme in the novel. Characters have the willpower to overcome obstacles and stay on the track leading to their goals. Whether it is commanding a battle, positively responding to an urgent call in the name of justice and freedom, relying on friends or engaging in perilous missions, determination invests characters with the fortitude to never surrender or retreat before any impediments.

Bravery is a defining trait of the heroes in *The Ventara Adventures*. They must shake off their fears (if any) and risk their lives to achieve objectives. From daring rescues to grand fights, characters display inspirational acts of bravery. The novel leaves us with a gratifying, stirring aftertaste coming from a powerful sci-fi chronicle that strikes home in a broad range of viewer ages. With the themes of hope in the face of gloom, determination in the midst of tests, and heroism in the struggle against injustice, this story teaches us to have confidence in a brighter tomorrow.

Altogether, *The Ventara Adventures: The Resilience of Hope* may be deemed epic and stimulating for those who will see themselves connected to it. Their personal association will surely be based on theme and subtheme variety, the humanness of the characters and the grand battles fought, which arouse the readers and might even make them think of themselves as heroes, at least on a smaller, more-down-to-earth scale; nonetheless, relevant in their own lives.

The euphoria and optimism about the future the author ably transmits to the readers is palpable across the pages. Again, and always, hope, resilience, invincible spirits, enthusiasm, positivity and minds set on what is ahead, colour the novel and bring solidity to a story that should be told many times because the human kind needs its message, its greatness and its warning; a warning that in the book is epitomized by Virox, but there are also numberless threats around the corner of our lives and our world.

Also across the novel´s pages we will take delight in the words of the romantic writer, the hopeful, optimistic author, who leaves for us lines of sheer tenderness and expectation; lines that reinforce the notions of determination and hope.

Hans Müller is a devoted believer in hope and life. His commitment transpires in his story, so as readers we plunge headlong into the fast-forward events playing out before our avid eyes, the vigor of the people who make them happen and the intensity of their actions to right the wrongs. Müller views hope in the terms below:

"Through hope, the human spirit navigates the complexities of existence, ever resilient, ever reaching for the horizon of possibility."

I feel the urge to close my review quoting from a humble sci-fi short story, "Farewell," I published years ago. In many ways, it approaches and embraces Müller´s priceless ideas about hope:

"The ship flared, lifted the silvery body with its precious cargo and swiftly crossed the atmosphere. Behind it, a dying planet and a promising farewell wake signaling a voyage into obscure infinity that would harvest hopes of renewed life." In my words I projected Müller´s horizon of possibility, which we have to ever-expand and safeguard sanguinely, expectantly.

Therefore, I invite readers to pilot a spaceship, escort Kael and his friends, go on a mission to save Princess Quann and put their lives on the line for a victory that will always be welcome, will always be worth going after, for it means peace and prosperity for the people, here on our dear planet or anywhere in the unfathomable expanses of the cosmos.

Thank you, Hans.

Preface from the Author

Hope and the idea of the expectancy of good are intangible yet profoundly influential forces that stand resilient amid the vicissitudes of life. It is an ember that refuses to extinguish, an inspiration guiding individuals through the toughest of times. Philosophically, hope is not merely a passive expectation for a better future but an active engagement with the present, infusing every moment with the potential for transformation and growth.

The resilience of hope is rooted in its capacity to transcend circumstances. In existential philosophy, hope is often seen as a response to the inherent uncertainties and absurdities of human existence. For thinkers like Kierkegaard, hope is a form of faith, a leap into the unknown, trusting that life holds meaning even when it is not immediately apparent. This resilience is not blind optimism but a conscious choice to confront despair with the belief in the possibility of a better outcome.

In the face of suffering and adversity, hope provides a lifeline, anchoring individuals to a sense of purpose and direction. Viktor Frankl, a psychiatrist and Holocaust survivor, emphasized that even in the direst conditions, the search for meaning—and the hope that accompanies it—can sustain the human spirit. His concept of "tragic optimism" highlights that hope does not deny the existence of suffering but rather affirms the potential for growth and meaning within it.

Moreover, hope is a communal phenomenon. It thrives in the shared aspirations and collective dreams of societies. Paulo Freire, a Brazilian educator and philosopher, viewed hope as a critical component of social change. For him, hope was an act of defiance against oppression, a necessary element for envisioning and working toward a more just and equitable world. It is in the collective pursuit of a better future that hope finds its most resilient expression.

Ultimately, the resilience of hope lies in its dynamic nature. It is not a static state but a continuous process of renewal and adaptation. It invites individuals to embrace uncertainty, to find strength in vulnerability, and to persist in the face of obstacles. Through hope, the human spirit navigates the complexities of existence, ever resilient, ever reaching for the horizon of possibility.

Expanding on this, the resilience of hope can be seen in the narrative of *The Ventara Adventures*, particularly in the character of Princess Quann. Despite being captured and held in Chancellor Virox's fortress, Princess Quann's unwavering hope becomes a beacon for her people and her rescuers. Her belief in the possibility of rescue and the eventual triumph over tyranny fuels her defiance and strategic planning even in the face of overwhelming odds.

Her hope is not passive; it is a driving force that propels her actions and inspires those around her. The message she manages to send, despite her captivity, symbolizes this active engagement with the present and the future. It is a testament to her resilience and the power of hope to transcend physical confines and oppressive circumstances.

The community aspect of hope is evident in the united efforts of Kael Ventara, Riz Talon, and

Mara Steeler. Their collective mission to rescue Quann embodies the communal nature of hope. Each member brings their unique strengths and unwavering belief in their cause, demonstrating how shared aspirations and collective dreams can lead to extraordinary feats of bravery and resistance.

In conclusion, the resilience of hope is a dynamic, communal, and transformative force. It enables individuals and societies to navigate life's uncertainties, find meaning in adversity, and strive for a better future. As demonstrated in *The Ventara Adventures*, hope's resilience lies in its ability to inspire, unite, and drive individuals toward their highest aspirations, even in the darkest of times.

Hans David Müller

Hope is the symphony of resilience
that plays
the melody of harmony.

Hope composes the music of endurance,
where resilience is the steady beat and
renewal is the uplifting harmony.
Together, they create a symphony
that echoes through the soul,
reminding us that no matter the dissonance we face,
a harmonious future is always possible.

Chapter 1

The Rise of Darkness

Radiant City, the capital of the Lumina Sector, is a bustling metropolis and a shining example of peace and progress in the galaxy. Its vibrant cities and lush landscapes have long been a haven of tranquility and prosperity. Citizens enjoy the benefits of advanced technology, cultural richness, and a strong sense of community. Wide boulevards lined with towering trees and vibrant flowers crisscross the city, connecting bustling marketplaces with serene residential areas. Children play in expansive parks, their laughter echoing through the air, while adults stroll along tree-shaded paths, enjoying the tranquility of nature interwoven with urban life. It has long been the envy and admiration of other Galactic Federation members.

In the heart of the city lies the Grand Park, an oasis of green amidst the urban landscape. Here, ancient trees spread their canopies wide, providing cool shade to picnickers and joggers alike. The park's centrepiece is a pristine lake, its surface sparkling under the midday sun. Families gather at its shores, feeding the colourful fish that dart just below the surface, while rowboats glide leisurely across the water, their occupants enjoying a peaceful respite from the city's hustle and bustle. Surrounding the lake, meticulously maintained gardens burst with colour, their blooms a testament to the Lumina Sector's commitment to the idea that beauty is interlocked with harmony and harmony promotes beauty.

Suddenly, the peace is disrupted by the distant roar of engines. Massive starships, dark and foreboding, cast long shadows over the city, their sleek, menacing designs a stark contrast to the vibrant life below. The once-clear skies are now filled with the ominous silhouettes of these enormous vessels, blocking out the sun and casting a pall over the cheerful cityscape. Known for its peaceful and prosperous civilizations, the Lumina Sector is thrown into turmoil as Virox's forces descend upon it with merciless precision.

It is the year 2165. With the approaching ships the galaxy teeters on the brink of intergalactic war. The malevolent Chancellor Virox, driven by his insatiable thirst for power, orchestrates a ruthless operation to capture Princess Quann of the Lumina Sector.

Princess Quann is not just a symbol of hope and prosperity but a strong leader and General of her home planet's military. With her shoulder length blonde hair that is easily tied back for action and a personality that embodies rebellion and strength, she is an inspiration of resistance against tyranny.

Panic spreads quickly through Radiant City. The joyous sounds of daily life are replaced by the blaring of emergency sirens and the urgent shouts of citizens seeking shelter. In the Grand Park, families abandon their picnics, and rowboats hastily return to the shore. The lake, which moments ago was a scene of serenity, now reflects the chaos above, its calm waters disturbed by the tremors of descending ships. Amidst the trees and gardens, people look to the skies with a mix of fear and disbelief, their peaceful lives shattered by the arrival of Virox's fleet.

* * *

General Thorne, of the Galactic Federation, a towering figure with a muscular build and a stern demeanor, urgently contacted Princess Quann on the Galactic Federation communication link. She calmly sits in her palace study room filled with books and paintings, "Princess Quann, I just received intel from one of our scout ships that Virox's fleet is approaching your city! Have you implemented your evacuation plans yet? As soon as we received the news I ordered squadrons of ships to assist you but even at warp nine our ships are still hours away. We can't give you immediate support. Your team must evacuate you to the Federation Headquarters on Earth immediately!"

Princess Quann stands with a sense of authority, "This is the first that I have heard but I will assemble the troops in Victory Square immediately. I will address them from the balcony. We will stand and fight. I will not abandon my people in their time of need."

The Royal Palace, a grand structure of shimmering white stone, is an image of peace and prosperity. Quann stands on a balcony overseeing the preparations as her soldiers ready their defences. The air is thick with tension.

Princess Quann turns to the image of General Thorne on the comm-system and splits the screen with General Martin, "General Martin, fortify the gates. Prepare the anti-aircraft defences. We will show Virox that the Lumina Sector does not fall easily."

General Thorne, despite his six-foot-four-inch muscular stature and normal confident demeanor looks worried, "Your Highness, we must prioritize your safety. If you fall, the Lumina Sector falls with you. Genereal Martin. Can't you talk some sense into Princess Quann."

Princess Quann thumps her fist into her open hand, "I will not hide. My place is with my people. Prepare the command centre; I will lead from there."

* * *

Chancellor Virox, a figure of legend and terror, has ruled with an iron fist for over fifty years. His rise to power was swift and ruthless, marked by cunning political maneuvers and brutal suppression of dissent. Born into a family of modest means on the war-torn planet of Kragnor, Virox demonstrated exceptional intelligence and ambition from a young age. He quickly rose through the ranks of the modest Kragnor military, earning a reputation as a brilliant strategist and a feared warrior. Now at the age of 110, through genetic manipulation and a rigid physical regime, he is a physically superior being with no sign of decline.

Under his rule, the galaxy has seen countless wars, with Virox's forces conquering and subjugating numerous sectors. His reign is characterized by oppression, fear, and relentless expansion. The Virox Empire, known as the Dark Dominion, stretches across vast regions of space, its influence felt on countless worlds. His regime has crushed rebellions and eliminated rivals with ruthless efficiency, leaving a legacy of fear and despair.

Virox's rise to power and the establishment of his empire were marked by strategic brilliance and ruthless ambition. He employed a combination of military might and psychological warfare to subjugate worlds. His tactics included the use of propaganda, espionage, and the systematic elimination of dissent. Virox's network of loyal followers and spies ensures that his control remains unchallenged. His regime is characterized by fear and oppression, but it is also efficient and orderly, with strict laws and harsh punishments for any who oppose him.

* * *

Within minutes of entering the Lumina atmosphere the skies above Radian City became a battlefield. The Virox starships, sleek and menacing, cut through the air. They deploy smaller fighter craft that dart towards the city, engaging the Lumina Sector's defences.

General Martin, a tall dignified man booms his voice over the intercom, "There are incoming enemy fighters breaching the security grid in south sector! Any available units engage! We must protect the Royal Palace at all cost!"

Chancellor Virox's cold and calculating voice echoes through all of the Virox ships, "Proceed with the plan. Capture the princess. That is our one and only goal, nothing else matters."

The command centre of the Royal Palace is a hive of activity. Princess Quann stands before a large tactical display, coordinating the defence. The room shakes as explosions rock the city.

Princess Quann points at the comm-screen with fear in her voice, "Hold the line! We cannot let them breach the inner defences."

A Galactic Federation Forces Officer runs to the side of Princess Quann, "Your Highness, Virox's ground troops have landed. They're making their way through the eastern quadrant."

Princess Quann grips her sword, "I'll meet them there. Secure the civilians. We will not let Virox's tyranny prevail."

* * *

The eastern quadrant of the city is a chaotic battlefield. Soldiers and civilians fight desperately against the invaders. Quann leads a charge, her sword gleaming in the sunlight.

Princess Quann raises her sword over her head and shouts to her troops, "For the Lumina Sector! For freedom!"

Troops echo, "For freedom, for freedom, for freedom!"

The battle is fierce. Quann fights with unparalleled skill and bravery, cutting through enemy ranks but Virox's forces are relentless, their numbers overwhelming. In a narrow alleyway near the palace, Quann, separated from her troops, faces a squad of Virox's elite soldiers. She fights valiantly but is eventually overpowered.

Virox soldiers bind her hands, "The Chancellor will be pleased. The princess is captured."

Princess Quann, in a loud menacing voice, "You may capture me, but you will never break the spirit of my people."

* * *

The Virox command ship, the Dominator, is a fortress in space. Chancellor Virox watches a holographic feed of Princess Quann's capture, a sinister smile on his face.

Chancellor Virox raises his fists in victory, "Excellent. With the princess in our grasp, the galaxy will bow to our will. Prepare her for transport. We leave at once."

* * *

Back on earth the Galactic Federation Headquarters, a sprawling complex of tall buildings and hanger bays buzzes with activity. It is thrown into chaos as the news of Princess Quann's capture spreads like wildfire.

Ambassador Zane, from the GF Headquarters, with a tone of defiance broadcasts a message, "This is a dark day for the Galactic Federation and the galaxy in general. Princess Quann's capture threatens the very fabric of the entire alliance. We must act swiftly to rescue her and thwart Chancellor Virox's plans."

Council Members, with a hushed tone turn to each other, "Who will lead this mission? We need someone with the skill and bravery to face Virox."

Ambassador Zane replies to the muttering Council, "There is one who can. We must summon Kael Ventara. He withdrew from the GFF a couple of years ago, but he was the best pilot the GFF has ever had. We have been in a state of peace for so many years that we don't have a single trained pilot that even comes close to his skills. General Thorne, send your troops out to find him immediately."

* * *

Kael Ventara, once a celebrated pilot and hero of the Galactic Federation Forces, now lives in self-imposed exile on the desolate planet of Duneara. His withdrawal from the military was driven by disillusionment and a desire to escape the constant battles and politically motivated strategic orders. Kael's past is filled with tales of bravery and skill, but he now spends his days in solitude, far from the conflicts that once defined his life.

It was the battle of Zarath Prime that was the turning point that led Captain Ventara to leave the Galactic Federation Forces. Even though he was a celebrated pilot he found himself at the forefront of a decisive conflict against the forces of Traylack. The battle was fierce, with starships clashing in a deadly ballet. Captain Kael led his squadron against superior number and superior ships against the Traylack forces, but as the battle progressed, he witnessed the true impetus of the Federation's political plotting and scheming. Orders from high command, tainted by ulterior motives, led to unnecessary losses and collateral damage from friendly fire. Innocent lives were sacrificed for political strategic gains. From that point on the once-clear lines between right and wrong were forever blurred.

In the heart of the battle Kael watched in horror as civilian colonies were caught in the crossfire, their pleas for mercy ignored by his superiors. The final straw came when he received an order to abandon a contingent of his own men to ensure what was later called a vital political victory. Over time his conscience couldn't bear the weight of these decisions. Disillusioned and heartbroken, Kael resigned his commission and buried his disappointment in the Federation's brass. The aftermath left him questioning everything he had believed in and fought for.

Seeking to escape the constant mental battles he chose self-imposed exile on the desolate planet of Duneara. There, far from the conflicts of war that once defined his life, he sought solace and a chance to heal from the scars of war. His past was filled with tales of bravery and skill, but he was constantly haunted by the memories of Zarath Prime.

With the galaxy plunged into chaos as Chancellor Virox's dark plans came to fruition. Princess Quann's capture was a devastating blow to the forces of good, but her defiant spirit remained unbroken. As the call for a hero echoed across the stars, the stage was set for Kael Ventara to rise to the challenge. Despite his desire for peace of mind, the call to rescue Princess Quann drew him back into the fray.

Embarking on a daring mission to rescue the princess, Kael would once again become a beacon of hope in the epic saga of bravery, rebellion, and the timeless struggle between good and evil. The galaxy awaited its hero. Was Kael Ventara emotionally ready to come out of hiding and answer the call?

Hope is the sunrise
after the longest night.

Darkness may last, but it is never permanent.
Hope assures us that dawn is inevitable,
no matter how long the night.
Just as the sun rises after the deepest darkness,
hope promises renewal and light,
reminding us that every end holds the potential
for a new beginning.

Chapter 2
The Hero's Awakening

The desert planet of Duneara, known as the armpit of the galaxy for its harsh and unforgiving climate, stretches out under a sky with three 24 hour relentless suns. The temperature soars to scorching heights, often reaching 120 °F, making the landscape a hostile environment for any form of life. The barren dunes roll endlessly, occasionally interrupted by jagged rock formations and sparse, hardy vegetation that stubbornly clings to life. The hot winds whip across the dunes, carrying fine sand that stings the skin and gets into every crevice, a constant reminder of the planet's merciless nature.

The only reason anyone would bother setting foot on this waterless perilous planet was the rare and expensive Arbite Ore that lay just below the sandy surface. The entire planetary infrastructure was based on Arbite. You were either a sand clearer, an Arbite driller, an Arbite loader, an Arbite shipper or you supplied those workers with all of the needed goods and services that kept the Arbite flowing.

Amidst this desolate backdrop lives Kael Ventara, an Arbite digger, a celebrated twenty-seven-year-old former pilot and skilled swordsman of the Galactic Federation Forces (GFF). Kael now leads a solitary life, far from the battles and politics of the galaxy that once defined him. He has rugged features, with tousled brown hair that falls just above his piercing green eyes, often shadowed by a hint of fatigue. His tanned skin reflects the harsh sun of Duneara, and a few scars tell stories of past battles. Kael's lean, muscular build speaks to his rigorous training and adventurous past, but now if he is not running an Arbite digger he spends his days tinkering with his old starship, finding solace in the hobby of mechanical work.

Kael's modest home is a stark contrast to the vast emptiness outside. The interior is cluttered with tools, starship parts, and various mechanical devices, all remnants of a past life filled with purpose and adventure. The walls are adorned with faded posters of the GFF and old photos of comrades from battles long past. A small, well-worn couch sits in one corner, facing a simple table cluttered with schematics and notes. Despite the disorder, there is a sense of familiarity and comfort in the chaos.

One sweltering afternoon, as Kael worked on his starship, the Starfire, sweat dripped from his brow. The suns blazed overhead, casting sharp shadows on the arid landscape. The Starfire, once a gleaming symbol of his prowess, now showed signs of wear and tear. Its hull is marked with scorch marks and scratches from countless skirmishes. Kael is crouched under the ship, tightening a bolt, when the silence is broken by the sudden, urgent beeping of a distress signal.

Startled, Kael moves quickly to the comm-panel inside his makeshift hangar, "What in the galaxy?" he mutters, activating the panel.

The message crackles through the static, bringing with it an urgency that Kael hasn't felt in years, "This is a priority-one message from the Galactic

Federation. All available forces are to report immediately. Princess Quann has been captured by Chancellor Virox. We need your help, Kael Ventara. You are our only hope."

Kael's eyes widened. The names 'Princess Quann' and 'Chancellor Virox' were pulling him back into a world he had tried to leave behind. Kael muttered to himself, "Quann... Virox... I knew this day would eventually come. Somehow, someone would pull the strings like I was a puppet and I would be dragged back into the chaos of political wars," he grumbled to himself. As he stared at the message on the computer screen, the sound of a military CX7 Airwing landing close to his house and filled the air with dust and sand in every direction. He knows instinctively that an envoy has been dispatched to ensure he starts packing for his assignment. He continues to talk to himself in a soft voice, "Once in the military, always in the military. They don't tell you to read the fine print that they can pull you back in at any time."

It only took a moment for Kael to make his decision to comply, "I guess I can't hide out on this hot dust bowel of a planet forever." Kael laughs, "I guess I was destined to rescue a princess at least once in my life, now is as good a time as any." He heads to a dusty storage room, where his old GFF uniform hung. He pulls it out of its dusty plastic cover, the sight of it bringing a flood of memories. It was as if he had hung it there only yesterday. With a resigned look on his face, he puts the uniform up to his chest and speaks to the mirror, "Time to get back in the fight, you lazy lug."

As Kael continues to pack, his mind races with memories of his years in the GFF. He recalls the camaraderie, the battles, and the sense of purpose that once drove him. Each item that he packs; a GFF issued blaster pulled from a plastic bag, a data pad filled with tactical information flickers to life as if it had been used just yesterday, and a small, tattered photograph of his squad, all serve as a reminder of the life he left behind. He can feel the weight of responsibility settling back onto his shoulders, mingled with a sense of duty and honour that he thought he had left behind.

Kael mutters to himself, "I never thought I'd return," Kael shakes sand from his hair and says aloud, "But if there's a chance that I can help to save Princess Quann and stop Virox from one more conquest then, I have to do this. Where are my black military boots?"

A voice calls from the living room, "Captain Ventara, are you packing? I have strict orders not to leave until I have helped load your gear into your starship." There is a long pause, "Captain, can I help you with anything?"

* * *

Outside, the relentless sun glares down as Kael makes his way to his starship. He climbs aboard, the familiar hum of the engines bringing a sense of purpose and urgency, "Alright, old girl," he says, activating the ship's systems, "Let's see if you've still got some fight left in you."

The Starfire lifts off, leaving the desolate landscape of Duneara behind. As he ascends into space, Kael sets a course for the Federation Headquarters, his resolve hardening with each passing moment. The barren planet quickly recedes, replaced by the vast, star-filled expanse of space. Kael watches as the coordinates for the Galactic Federation Headquarters lock into place on his navigation screen. His mind is a whirlwind of thoughts and emotions, the urgent call for help resonating deeply within him.

The journey to the Federation Headquarters gave Kael time to reflect on his past. As the Starfire glides through the vast expanse of space, memories flood his mind, each one vivid and poignant. He recalls his early days in the GFF, fresh out of the academy, brimming with ambition and eager to prove himself. Those days were a whirlwind of training exercises and first missions, each one testing his skills and pushing him to his limits. He remembers the adrenaline rush of his first combat flight, the sharp focus required to outmaneuver enemies, and the immense satisfaction of a mission accomplished.

Friendships were forged in the crucible of battle, bonds that were as strong as they were sudden. He thinks of Riz Talon, with his boisterous laugh and unyielding bravery, and Mara Steeler, whose tough exterior hid a heart of gold. Together, they faced insurmountable odds, their camaraderie a vital element in their survival and success. These friendships, tempered by the fires of war, became a source of strength and solace.

Kael vividly recalls the Battle of Eridia Prime, a mission that went disastrously wrong. They were ambushed by a superior enemy force hiding in an asteroid cluster. Kael and his squad were on their way home after what was supposed to be a simple reconnaissance mission. He lost three of his closest comrades that day. Jax, Marc and Marlo, all veteran pilots. Jax's fighter exploded in a ball of fire after enemy fire caught them off guard. Marc and Marlo fought valiantly taking out four enemy gunners. Marlo's final words over the comm, "Get out of here while you can. Marc and I both have shot up ships and won't make it home. We will hold them off as long as we can and do as much damage as possible. Get back to the base with the important data we gathered. Take care, buddy." Those last words still echo in his mind. The pain of losing them, their sacrifices etched into his heart, serves as a constant reminder of the brutal reality of war that he thought he had escaped from.

Kael knows only too well that all memories are not joyful. His mind drifts to other losses that left indelible scars on his soul. Comrades who fell in battle, their sacrifices haunting him. Each loss was a reminder of the brutal reality of war, the price of peace and freedom. These memories are a stark contrast to the victories, a somber reflection of the cost of their struggle.

His thoughts inevitably turn to Princess Quann. He remembers her fierce determination, her unwavering spirit in the face of adversity. Princess Quann was more than just a symbol of hope for the Lumina Sector; she embodied the resilience and strength that represented the Galactic Federation. Her leadership was a beacon, guiding them through the darkest times. She inspired loyalty and courage, qualities that made her not just a leader, but someone worth fighting for. For Kael, rescuing her isn't just a mission—it's a reaffirmation of everything they fought for, a chance to fight for personal choices and not governed by autocracy and oppression.

* * *

The Galactic Federation Headquarters is a sprawling complex buzzing with activity. As Kael's starship descends, he is greeted by the sight of old comrades and new faces alike. The air is thick with the urgency of the mission ahead. Kael heads to the briefing room, where high-ranking officials await his arrival.

General Thorne, a towering figure with a stern demeanor, steps forward, "Captain Ventara, it's good to have you back. We need your skills now more than ever."

Kael nods, his expression thoughtful, "I'm here to help. What's the situation?"

Ambassador Zane, projecting a holographic map of the galaxy, points to a location marked with a bright red dot, "Princess Quann is being held on Virox's command ship, heavily guarded. We need a skilled pilot to lead the rescue mission. That's where you come in."

Kael studies the map, his eyes narrowing with determination, "I'll get her back. You have my word."

The briefing continues, with detailed discussions on the mission's objectives and potential obstacles. Kael listens intently, absorbing every piece of information. The stakes are high, and the margin for error is slim. He knows that success will depend not only on his skills but also on the coordination and bravery of the entire team.

* * *

The training facility at the Federation Headquarters is a state-of-the-art complex designed to hone the skills of its operatives. While the Federation Headquarters gathers needed intel, Kael undergoes rigorous retraining, honing his skills and preparing for the mission. He spars with combat droids, practices his swordsmanship, and refines his piloting techniques. The relentless training pushes him to his limits, but he welcomes the challenge, finding a revitalized goal in the familiar routines.

A training officer watches Kael spar with a combat droid, his movements fluid and precise, "You haven't lost your touch, Ventara. Impressive."

Kael turned to the raining officer and said, It's not like I have been sitting on my butt. You always have to be on the ball when you live on a sand-pit, hell-hole like Duneara. If you are not defending your property and goods from scavengers you are fighting off one-eyed sand serpents. You have to have your blaster with you at every moment. They sneak up on you breathing heavily, wipes sweat from his brow, "I've had a lot of time to think out there. It's good to be back in action."

The training sessions are intense, each designed to prepare Kael for the various scenarios he might face during the rescue mission. He acquaints himself with new advanced flight maneuvers, practices close-quarter combat, and participates in simulations that test his strategic thinking under pressure. The days are long and grueling, but with each passing hour, Kael feels more like his old self: confident, capable, and ready to take on any challenge.

* * *

Back in the briefing room, Kael and the senior officers gather for the final mission briefing. The room is filled with tension, the stakes high. Ambassador Zane addresses the room, his voice steady and authoritative.

"This mission won't be as easy as the whiteboard suggests it will be. Virox's defences will be difficult to penetrate, and he won't hesitate to use Quann as leverage but with Captain Kael leading us, we at least have a fighting chance."

General Thorne stands, his gaze sweeping over the faces of everyone in the briefing room, "There is only one way to do this, we go in fast. No time to look behind us. We do our job, and we get out quick. Stick to your training, trust your instincts, and we'll make it through. Before we finish is there anything that anyone feels we have left out."

The team responds with nods of fortitude and murmurs of agreement. Each member is handpicked for their unique skills and unwavering loyalty. They understand the risks involved and the importance of their mission. The room buzzes with a mixture of apprehension and resolve, the weight of their task pressing heavily on their shoulders.

With a sense of nervousness Kael stands and clears his throat to get everyone's attention, "Excuse me General Thorne, can I have a few words? I think that you have assembled a wonderful team to carry out the mission but with all due respect I have to request that I be allowed to pick and manage my own team."

General Thorne tells everyone to sit back down and stop talking, "Captain Ventara, what do you mean pick your own team? What do you think is wrong with this team that Ambassador Zane and I have assembled? They are the best combat officers that we have. Between them and the starship that is being readied as we speak, you will have the Galactic best to work with."

Kael stays standing at ease, hands gripped at his back, "With all due respect General, not a single one of the team you have assembled have any combat experience. The Federation has been in a state of peace for so many years that, I have to say, these people are all a bit green and will crumble at the first sight of blasters firing at them. What I would like is to bring former First Lieutenant Riz Talon and Former Second Lieutenant Mara Steeler as my team."

General Thorne frowned, "Are you telling me that you just want two team members, both of them not even in active duty, when you can have this team of eight?"

Kael stood at attention, "Sir, yes, Sir. It is my opinion that, smaller with more skill is the way to go with this mission, Sir. And Sir, I would respectfully request that I use my own starship for the mission. The Starfire is smaller and more maneuverable than the B67 that you are suggesting."

Everyone in the room is starting to murmur and look around at each other. Ambassador Zane stands and looks directly into Kael's eyes, "I remember Talon and Steeler, they were the best Lieutenants we ever had. If you can contact them and get them mission ready within a few days then you can have them and your Starfire. Get on to it and report to General Thorne by 0200 tomorrow. If your team and ship are not ready in time we are moving out with or without you with our B67 and our eight men."

* * *

The call to duty has reignited Kael's spirit, and he is ready to face whatever dangers lie ahead. The rescue mission is fraught with peril, but Kael Ventara, once a hero of the Galactic Federation, is back in the fight. His mission to save Princess Quann has begun, setting the stage for the epic battles and adventures that will follow. He punches in the coordinates for the planet Zauron to find Riz and Mara. He sits back with his feet up.

Hope in the darkest nights
is the star that never fades.

In life's darkest hours,
hope remains our constant guide.
Like a star,
it provides direction when all other lights fail.
Hope endures through hardship,
illuminating the path forward
even when the journey is uncertain and
the destination seems unreachable.

Chapter 3

Allies in the Stars

Kael Ventara sat in the cockpit of the Starfire, studying the holographic star charts displayed before him. The holograms projected intricate maps of the galaxy, with shimmering dots representing planets, stars, and other celestial bodies. Each point of light pulsed gently, indicating their coordinates and relevant data. Lines connected the dots, tracing possible flight paths and routes across the vast expanse of space. The charts were detailed and complex, filled with layers of information that only an experienced pilot like Kael could decipher with ease.

To successfully rescue Princess Quann, Kael knew he would need the help of his old military friends.

Determined, he set the course for the distant planet of Zauron, where they had agreed to meet years ago if they ever needed each other again. Hope beyond hope was his only hope. How much time had it been since he saw Riz and Mara. What made him think that they would still be on Zauron after all of this time. What made him think that he could just waltz in and find them even if they were on the planet? The memories of their shared promise brought a sense of purpose and urgency to his mission. As the Starfire streaked across the galaxy, Kael's mind was filled with memories of battles fought and bonds forged.

The Starfire cut through the void of space, its engines humming steadily as Kael guided it toward Zauron. The familiar controls beneath his fingers and the soft hum of the ship's systems were comforting, almost meditative, as he journeyed through the vast expanse. The stars outside streaked past like elongated diamonds against the blackness, a sight he had seen countless times yet never grew tired of.

Kael reflected on the many missions they had undertaken together, the camaraderie that had been their strength. Riz Talon and Mara Steeler had been more than just comrades; they were family. He remembered their laughter, their fierce loyalty, and the unwavering trust they had in one another. Riz, with his gruff exterior and endless supply of war stories, had a way of lightening even the most tense situations. His mechanical genius and fearless spirit made him an invaluable ally. Mara, tough yet compassionate, was the strategic mind of their group, always thinking several steps ahead. Her sharp instincts and unyielding courage had saved them more times than Kael could count.

Kael's mind wandered into the past. He remembered a time when they had been dispatched to the remote and perilous planet of Thaloria, a world infamous for its treacherous terrain and hostile wildlife. Their mission was to extract a high-value target, an undercover agent who had crucial intelligence about an impending attack by Chancellor Virox's forces. The stakes were high, and failure was not an option.

As they descended through the thick, storm-laden atmosphere, their shuttle was struck by wave from a plasma storm, sending them spiraling out of control. Riz, with his unparalleled mechanical skills, managed to stabilize the craft just enough to make a rough landing in the dense jungle. The memory of the crash landing, the shrieking metal, and the gut-wrenching drop still sent chills down Kael's spine.

Once on the ground, they were immediately beset by Thaloria's dangerous flora and fauna. Mara, ever the strategist, quickly took charge, organizing their defensive perimeter and setting traps to fend off the predatory creatures that lurked in the shadows. Her quick thinking and calm under pressure had saved them from being overrun. Kael could still hear her sharp commands and see the resolute in her eyes as she directed their efforts.

As they made their way through the jungle, they faced relentless attacks and natural hazards. Riz's expertise kept their equipment functioning despite the damp and corrosive environment, while Mara's tactical acumen ensured they stayed on course and avoided the worst of the dangers. Kael's role was to keep their spirits high, using his flying skills to scout ahead and his combat prowess to protect his team.

The extraction itself was a blur of gunfire, narrow escapes, and heart-pounding moments. They had found the agent held up in a makeshift shelter, wounded but alive. The return journey was no less harrowing, with Virox's patrols hot on their heels. In the end, they managed to evade capture and deliver the intelligence, thwarting a major attack that could have devastated the Federation.

Each mission had strengthened their bond, forging an unbreakable connection. They had seen each other at their best and their worst, and that deep-seated trust was something Kael knew he could rely on. The thought of reuniting with them filled him with a reborn sense of hope. For Princess Quann and the sake of the galaxy, they would fight together once more, just as they had on Thaloria. Together, they had faced insurmountable odds, from daring rescues to intense dogfights in space. Each mission had strengthened their bond, forging an unbreakable connection.

As Zauron grew closer on the navigation screen, Kael's determination solidified. He knew the mission ahead would be dangerous, but with Riz and Mara by his side, he believed they could overcome any obstacle. For Princess Quann and for the sake of the galaxy, he hoped he would find them and find them well. Kael knew it was a presumptuous that they would want to join him on this mission but he had to ask.

* * *

Arriving at Zauron, Kael descended into the atmosphere, guiding the Starfire toward a bustling spaceport on the rugged planet. The port was a hive of activity, filled with starships of all kinds from over a dozen planets. The air buzzed with the hum of machinery and the chatter of countless beings. Vendors called out their wares, mechanics clanged tools against metal, and the sounds of distant engines revved adding to the cacophony. The spaceport was a melting pot of species and cultures, each contributing to the vibrant, chaotic atmosphere.

Kael navigated through the crowded streets. He had no idea if Riz and Mara were even on the planet let alone in this location. All he had to go on was an unsubstantiated hunch. His eyes scanning for familiar faces, "Excuse me, aren't you Bob the mechanic? I haven't seen you in ages. Do you remember Riz and Mara? By chance have you seen them lately?" Without pausing to let Bob answer he continued, "I just had an intuitive sense that I should come here and look for them. It's

kind of important that I find them right away."
The spaceport was a bustle of people moving in
every direction. Without saying a word Bob
pointed down the street behind Kael. He turned
around and there was Riz Talon and Mara Steeler
near a busy docking bay walking towards him.

Kael turned around back to Bob and laughed,
"That's amazing, thanks."

Bob grunted, "You're welcome but I didn't do
anything."

"Riz! Mara! Over here!" Kael called out, his voice
cutting through the noise.

Riz, a tall and muscular mechanic with a wild
mane of hair, turned and grinned widely, "Kael,
you old dog! Look at you, still as dashing as ever.
What in the galaxy are you doing here?"

Mara, a tough yet kind-hearted former soldier,
punched Kael hard on the chest, "We were talking
about you just the other day. We figured that you
might have forgotten about us. Good to see you,
you old one-eyed sand serpent."

Kael laughed, feeling a wave of nostalgia wash over him, "Forgotten about you two? Never. How could I forget about you when I've got a mission, and I need the best. Are you available?"

Riz clapped Kael on the back, his eyes gleaming with excitement, "You bet we are you old bone head. What's the plan?"

Mara pushed Riz aside, "What do you mean we are available. You are the bone head you old bone head. You didn't even ask what the mission was. Just because he is your buddy and you are glad to see him even though you haven't seen hide for hair of him for eons, doesn't mean you have to jump in his lap like a starving squirrel monkey. Don't you remember that he just about got us all killed over a dozen times including our last mission. Tell me you remember the eight foot tall Saskeean who picked you up by the neck and was about to lick off your face with his green acid tongue and Kael where was he, he was on his back pretending to be a bull rider."

Kael clapped Riz on the back and said, "Thanks Riz buddy. Have you been feeding Mara sour goose berries again. You know she gets grumpy when she has a sour stomach. Mara you know perfectly well that I was on the back of that Saskean because I wanted to pock him in he eyes because that is the only soft spot on their entire body. You calling him a bone head? If you didn't have the mush-brain of a baby Saskean I would call you a bone-head."

Kael, Riz and Mara laughed and clapped each other on the backs.

Kael's expression grew serious, "I'm so glad that I found you so quickly. It's urgent. We're going to rescue Princess Quann but first, we need to get the Starfire to the GFF base for refitting and us for briefing. We only have two days to get in shape before we head out. The Starfire has been sitting idle for too long. How are you guys doing. Are you in shape?"

Mara nodded, and rolled her eyes as if they were all crazy, "We've got a pretty little princess to save. Kael is a baboon in heat so we all gotta jump and say how high. Kael, do you have a plan? Do you even know where she is being held captive?"

Riz put his two thumbs up, "Who cares about all that planning crap for now. We're in pretty good shape and that's all that matters. We have been security for a freight hauler since we left the GFF. We end up in a few skirmishes just about every trip so our trigger fingers are in pretty good shape.

* * *

The Starfire's hull was a testament to the ship's many adventures. The vessel, while sturdy, showed signs of neglect. Its once-shiny hull was now dulled with blaster scorch marks and asteroid scrapes, the wear and tear from countless missions was evident in the form of dents and scratches. Riz, Mara, and Kael set to work, their banter lightening the atmosphere as they repaired and upgraded the Starfire with the limited resources they had.

Riz wiped sweat from his brow, his hands covered in grease, "She's going to need a better upgrade than I can give her here but at least we will make her space worthy. Remember the time we took on that pirate fleet? That was something, huh?"

Kael glanced up from the engine core he was working on, a smile tugging at the corners of his mouth, "How could I forget? We were outnumbered ten to one, and our shields were down to 30%."

Mara, who was tightening some bolts on a manifold nearby, chuckled, "And let's not forget, we had just come out of a skirmish with Virox's patrols. The Starfire was barely holding together. You remember all of this and you two bone heads still want to head off and save a pretty little princess. You are more crazy than I thought."

Riz leaned back against the ship's hull, his eyes distant as he recalled the extreme battle, "Yeah, and they came at us from all sides. We were in the middle of that asteroid field, using every bit of cover we could find."

Kael nodded, his mind replaying the chaotic dogfight, "I remember dodging those asteroids, trying to shake off the pirate fighters. Riz, you were down in the engine room, practically holding things together with duct tape and prayers."

Riz laughed, "Damn right. I was rerouting power from life support to the weapons systems. We had to give it everything we had."

Mara's eyes sparkled with the memory, "And then, Kael, you pulled that crazy maneuver, spinning the Starfire through that narrow gap between two asteroids. We lost three of their ships in the collision."

Kael grinned, "Desperate times call for desperate measures. And Mara, your marksmanship took out their lead ship's engines. That was the turning point."

Riz nodded, "We barely made it out, but we did it together. We took down a pirate fleet with sheer grit and teamwork. Once again it reminds me of your motto – One impossible mission at a time."

Kael looked at his friends, feeling a deep sense of pride and camaraderie, "We were a hell of a team. And we still are. Let's get this bird ready. We've got another impossible mission to tackle." Kael smirked, checking to make sure that the manifold on the modulator was tight, "Hey, it worked, didn't it? We took them down and lived to tell the tale."

Riz shook his head, smiling, "Crazy times. We've all gotten a bit soft since then, haven't we?"

Mara sighed, a hint of nostalgia in her voice, "Yah great times. That was almost-dead number twenty. Great times. I was hoping to tell some of these stories to my grandkids. Two years out of the Federation, and I feel like I've aged a decade. But this working on the Starfire, getting ready for another mission, it feels right. I guess I am ready to rescue a pretty little princess with you Kael."

Kael's resolve was almost tangible, "We may have been out of action for a while, but we're still the best. And we're going to prove it."

* * *

The cockpit of the Starfire, now repaired and upgraded to the best they could do, felt like home to the three friends. They sat together, ready to take off. The controls hummed softly under Kael's hands, the ship responding smoothly to his touch.

Kael checked the controls one last time, "All systems go. Course set for Federation training. Let's take her out past the second star to the right and straight on 'til morning. You two ready?"

Riz grinned, his excitement infectious, "Born ready. Let's do this."

Mara smiled, her eyes shining with anticipation, "Time to show the galaxy what we're made of."

Kael nodded, feeling a rekindled sense of purpose, "Alright, Starfire. Let's see what you've got."

The Starfire lifted off smoothly, soaring into the sky and beyond, leaving Zauron behind. As they broke through the atmosphere and entered the vast expanse of space, the sense of camaraderie and purpose among the crew was profound. The familiar stars stretched out before them, twinkling like countless diamonds scattered across a velvet canvas. Each star held the promise of new adventures and distant planets waiting to be explored. Nebulas glowed with ethereal beauty in the distance, and the faint outlines of far-off galaxies hinted at the vastness of the universe. The crew felt an exciting feeling of wonder as they ventured into the cosmic frontier.

* * *

On route to the Federation training facility, the crew relaxed and caught up on old times. The ship's autopilot was engaged, allowing them a brief respite from the intensity of non-stop work on the ship.

Riz leaned back in his seat, a contented smile on his face, "It's good to be back in action. I missed the thrill, the adventure."

Mara nodded in agreement, her expression thoughtful, "And the company. We've been through a lot together. This mission. It feels like old times."

Kael smiled, a sense of pride swelling in his chest, "It does and we're going to need every bit of that old magic to pull this off. Princess Quann is counting on us."

Riz's determination was evident in his voice, "Then let's not let her down. To the Starfire, and to us—back in the game."

Mara raised an imaginary glass, her eyes sparkling with resolve, "To us. Let's make history."

Kael felt a surge of gratitude for his friends, "It is so great to have you on board. I was not sure I wanted to head into battle without you guys."

* * *

As the Starfire sped towards its destination at warp speed, the crew's bond was strengthened, their will steadfast. They were ready to face whatever challenges came their way, united in their mission to rescue Princess Quann and defeat Virox once and for all.

The familiar hum of the engines and the gentle vibrations of the ship were comforting, a reminder of the countless missions they had undertaken together. Each member of the team brought unique skills and strengths, creating a synergy that made them a intimidating force.

Kael's mind drifted back to the day they had agreed to meet on Zauron if they ever needed each other again. It had been a pact made in the heat of battle, a promise to always have each other's backs. And now, as they embarked on this new mission, that promise held true. It was a promise of cosmic order. The fact that Kael found Riz and Mara without a hitch proved their intergalactic connection.

Hope is the future that we make possible.

Hope is not passive;
it is an active force that lives inside us,
beyond our human preparation.
It shapes our tomorrow.
By believing in a better future
we summon the courage needed
to build what is yet to come,
beyond what we can accomplish by will alone.

Chapter 4

Training for the Trio

The Galactic Federation training facility was a sprawling complex, a hub of activity and preparation. Sleek buildings rose from the ground, interconnected by glass arched bridges and hedge-lined walkways and bustling with personnel. As the Starfire descended, Kael's heart swelled with a mixture of anticipation and resolve. This was the beginning of a new chapter, a chance to make a difference once more.

As the ship touched down, Kael spotted a troop of cadets marching by in perfect formation, their crisp uniforms gleaming in the sunlight. The cadets moved with a practiced precision, but their youthful features betrayed their inexperience. Kael watched them intently, reminiscing his own days as a fresh recruit.

"Look at how young they are," Kael murmured, almost to himself, "They are like boys. Were we ever that young and green?"

Riz, standing beside him, nodded thoughtfully, "Yeah, we were. Seems like a lifetime ago now. They've got a lot to learn, but they'll get there. Just like we did."

Mara joined them, her gaze following the cadets as they marched past, "We were eager, just like them. Ready to take on the galaxy without a second thought. They'll face their trials, just as we did. And they'll grow from it."

Kael's resolve hardened as he watched the cadets disappear into one of the buildings. These young soldiers were the future of the Federation, and it was up to veterans like him to ensure they had a future worth fighting for. The sense of duty that had always driven him now felt more urgent than ever.

The crew was greeted by old comrades and new faces alike, the air thick with the urgency of the mission ahead. General Thorne, Ambassador Zane, and other high-ranking officials awaited their arrival, ready to provide the necessary briefings and support.

* * *

"Captain Ventara, it's good to have you back with Lieutenant Steeler and Lieutenant Talon," General Thorne said, his voice firm and reassuring, "I hope you three are in top shape. We need your skills now more than ever."

Kael nodded, his expression firm, "I have already done a couple of days of retraining but I would say we are in top shape and ready for action. How is our itinerary shaping up?

Ambassador Zane projected a holographic map of the galaxy, pointing to a strategic location, "Princess Quann is being held on Virox's command ship at the moment. She and the ship are heavily guarded but our intelligence suggests that they are taking her to the land base of Chancellor Virox's Royal Palace. It looks like the team of the three of you will be the perfect size for this new location. We need a skilled pilot and small team to execute this rescue mission. We are happy to have the three of you aboard. We will have heavily armed ships hidden in the asteroid maze ready to escort you out once you clear the Virox docking bay. There is no doubt that there will be plenty of Virox ships hot on your tail as soon as you try to blast off, "

Kael studied the map, his eyes narrowing with determination, "We'll get her back, Sir, or we will die trying. You have my word."

* * *

The training sessions for all three of them were intense, designed to hone their skills and prepare them for the challenges ahead. All three of them sparred with hovering combat droids that predicted their every move. Each session pushed them to their limits. All three of them grew in their confidence.

A training officer watched over them like a hawk to make sure they were ready in just thirty hours, "The three of you haven't lost your touch. As far as I am concerned you are as ready as you will ever be."

Kael, breathing heavily, wiped sweat from his brow, "I've had a lot of time to think while on my hot planet of Duneara. In some strange way it's good to be back in action."

The training facility buzzed with activity, each operative and backup teams worked tirelessly to prepare for the mission. The sense of camaraderie and shared purpose was palpable, creating a powerful atmosphere of resolve.

* * *

Back in the briefing room, Kael and the team of operatives gathered for the final mission analysis. The atmosphere was tense, the stakes high. Ambassador Zane addressed the team, his voice steady and authoritative.

"This mission won't be easy. Virox's defences are formidable, and he won't hesitate to use his entire resources to safeguard against infiltration but with Kael leading us, we have a fighting chance."

Kael looked hard over the entire team, "Our mission is to rescue the princess at all costs. There is no turning back once we have penetrated Virox's Royal Palace. You have all of the info you need so let's make it happen. I am confident that we'll make it in and out."

The team replied, "Yes Sir, we are ready Sir." Each member of the team was handpicked for their dogged loyalty. They understood the risks involved and the importance of the mission. The room buzzed with a mixture of apprehension and resolve, the weight of their task pressing heavily on their shoulders.

* * *

As the team assembled and prepared to launch, Kael stood at the helm of his starship, his resolve unwavering. The call to duty had reignited his spirit, and he was ready to face whatever dangers lay ahead. The rescue mission would be fraught with peril, but Captain Kael Ventara, once a hero of the Galactic Federation, was back in the fight. His journey to save Princess Quann had begun, setting the stage for the epic battles and adventures that would follow.

The Starfire's engines roared to life. The ship lifted off smoothly, soaring into the sky and beyond, leaving the training facility behind. As they broke through the atmosphere and entered the vast expanse of space, the sense of camaraderie and purpose among the crew was deep felt. The familiar stars stretched out before them, a reminder of the myriad adventures that waited.

Kael glanced at Riz and Mara, his heart swelling with appreciation and resolve. They were a team once more, ready to take on the galaxy's greatest challenges. The bond they shared was unbreakable, forged in the fires of battle and strengthened by years of unwavering loyalty.

"Alright guys. Let's see what this old bird can still do," Kael said, his voice filled with resolve.

As the Starfire sped towards its destination, the crew relaxed with a calm sense of purpose, their resolve steadfast. They were ready to face whatever challenges came their way. Their primary goal was to rescue Princess Quann and restore hope to the galaxy. The familiar hum of the engines and the gentle vibrations of the ship were comforting, a reminder of the many missions they had undertaken together. Each member of the team brought unique skills, creating a synergy that made them a formidable force.

The journey ahead was filled with uncertainty, but Kael knew they had what it took to succeed. The call to duty had reignited their spirits, and they were ready to face whatever dangers lay ahead. The rescue mission was fraught with peril, but Kael Ventara and his team were back in the fight, ready to make history once again.

Hope is the quiet whisper
that keeps us moving
through the silence of despair.

Despair silences the world,
yet hope speaks in whispers,
encouraging us to take one more step.
It doesn't need to shout;
its quiet assurance is enough to sustain us.
In the stillness of despair,
hope is the subtle force that propels us forward.

Chapter 5

Gilded Chains and Watchful Eyes

The low lit, gloomy command centre of Chancellor Virox's flagship, the Dominator, was filled with a tense, foreboding energy. Chancellor Virox, the malevolent ruler with an iron grip on the galaxy, stood before a vast holographic display of the galaxy, his cold eyes scanning the strategic points he aimed to control. His advisors and generals surrounded him, their faces reflecting a mixture of fear and respect as they awaited his commands.

Virox, his voice authoritative and cold, began to speak, "Deploy our fleets to these coordinates. I want every sector secured and every rebel cell eradicated. Leave no stone unturned."

General Bavin, a tall and imposing figure, nodded, "Yes, Chancellor. Our enforcer starships will begin the hunt immediately. Resistance will be crushed."

A smirk played on Virox's lips, "Good. The galaxy must learn that opposition is futile. Strengthen the planetary defences. No one must breach our strongholds."

General Bavin hesitated for a moment before speaking again, "Chancellor, what of Princess Quann? She remains defiant, despite our efforts."

Chancellor Virox's expression darkened, a twisted amusement in his eyes, "Ah, Princess Quann. Her spirit is admirable but ultimately vain. Continue to watch her closely. She will break eventually."

* * *

Within the opulent yet subtly oppressive quarters of Princess Quann, the stark contrast between luxury and captivity was ever-present. Despite the rich surroundings, the presence of guards and surveillance cameras served as constant reminders of her imprisonment. Princess Quann paced the room, her mind racing with thoughts of escape.

"They think they can break me with gilded chains and watchful eyes," she muttered to herself, "But I will not yield. There must be a way to signal the Federation."

Her thoughts were interrupted by the firm voice of a guard, "Princess, it is time for your meal. Please, sit."

Princess Quann composed herself and took a seat, maintaining her regal demeanor, "Thank you. Now, tell me, do you truly find satisfaction in serving a galactic tyrant? Does it not weigh heavily on your conscience that he governs with an iron fist, silencing any dissent with ruthless efficiency? What are your thoughts on his methods of ruling, where he mercilessly crushes the weak and seizes anything he desires to expand his empire? Can you honestly stand by such actions, knowing the suffering and injustice they bring to countless lives?"

The guard hesitated, avoiding her gaze, "My duty is to the Chancellor. It is not my calling to question the wisdom of our leader."

Quann's voice softened, conviction still in it, "Remember, even the mightiest walls can be brought down from within."

The guard, momentarily unsettled by her words, retreated, leaving Quann alone with her thoughts. She eyed the surveillance camera, masking her true intentions behind a composed facade.

* * *

In a secret meeting room within the Royal Palace, Virox's high-ranking officials gathered to discuss their strategies. Emotions ran high with tension.

General Bavin voiced his concerns, "Chancellor, the resistance grows bolder. Despite our efforts, they continue to disrupt our plans."

Chancellor Virox's anger flared, "Then we will crush them with overwhelming force. No act of rebellion will go unpunished. Double our patrols, increase the bounty on known rebels. Make an example of anyone who defies us."

General Bavin nodded confidently, "Understood, Chancellor. Our forces will ensure your will is carried out."

A sinister smile spread across Virox's face, "Excellent. And as for Princess Quann, continue to show her every courtesy. Let her see the futility of her defiance. Her people will not come for her. They are too afraid."

* * *

Later that evening, in the quiet of her quarters, Princess Quann once again seized the momentary distraction of the guards to search her surroundings. Every opportunity she had she looked in and behind dressers and cupboards, under rugs and behind paintings. During one of her rare moments when she thought she was not being watched, she looked behind a large tapestry hanging on one wall. Behind it she found a hidden panel that had been painted over. With a mix of excitement and caution over the next few days she managed to get it open. To her delight she found an old abandoned communication device. Hope beyond hope she wondered if it still worked.

"This could be it," she whispered to herself, "If I can just fix it and get a message out."

As she worked to activate the device, the sound of approaching footsteps caused her to hastily conceal her discovery and put away her makeshift screwdriver. She resumed her place, maintaining her exterior calm as the guard returned.

"Is everything alright, Princess?" the guard asked, suspicion in his eyes.

Quann smiled politely, "Yes, thank you. Just lost in thought."

* * *

In the grand hall of Virox's Royal Palace, the Chancellor addressed his commanders via a holographic projection. His towering figure flickered before them, radiating authority and menace. His message was long and tedious. It ended with, "Our grip on the galaxy tightens with each passing day. Continue your efforts. Soon, the entire galaxy will bow to our will, and any hope of rebellion will be but a distant memory."

The commanders saluted, their faces reflecting a mixture of fear and admiration, as Virox's image faded.

* * *

As the galaxy quaked under Virox's oppressive rule, the forces of oppression grew ever stronger. Yet, within the heart of Virox's stronghold, Princess Quann's spirit remained unbroken. Her silent defiance and strategic mind set the stage for a daring escape, as the hope for freedom continued to burn brightly, even in such circumstances.

Quann's nightly routines became more focused on her covert plans. She mapped out the guards' schedules, noting their patterns and shifts. Her mind was a constant whirl of strategies and potential escape routes. Each interaction with the guards, each glance at the surveillance cameras, was a part of her intricate plan.

One night, after another round of reconnaissance within her quarters, she managed to activate the hidden communication device. The screen flickered to life, displaying a series of encrypted codes. Quann quickly input a message, her fingers moving swiftly over the keys.

"To the Galactic Federation: If this message is received by friends of the Federation please contact the Federation HQ ASAP. This is Princess Quann. I am being held captive in Chancellor Virox's Royal Palace. I need immediate assistance. I will try to send another message with palace coordinates."

She pressed the button to send but it flickered and did not go. She fiddled with wires for a moment with no positive results. Afraid of being caught she closed the panel and returned the tapestry to its position. Her heart pounding with a mixture of fear and desperation.

* * *

In the depths of Virox's Royal Palace, an emergency meeting was convened. Virox's top advisors and generals gathered around a large, triangular table with Chancellor Virox at the apex. The dim lighting casting long shadows across their faces.

General Bavin spoke first, his tone earnest, "Chancellor, it seems that we have detected a spike in the comm-system. We don't know where it originated from but we suspect that it is from somewhere in the Royal Palace or the hanger bays. We are not sure and we are not overly concerned about it but I have men looking into it."

Virox's eyes narrowed, his voice cold and calculating, "General Bavin. It is not your job to be unconcerned. Keep your men on it until you find it."

General Bavin nodded, "Yes, Chancellor. I will report on our continued investigation." He saluted and stepped back.

Virox's lips curled into a menacing smile, "And how is our pretty little princess doing? I want her to receive every luxury that she desires. I want her to feel like she is a guest in the Royal Palace but keep her under lock and key at every moment. I want her to feel crushed after we take over her sweet little empire. We will strip it of all its resources and give it back to her in such a collapsed empty state that she will wish she had taken our offers to purchase her minerals when I offered. I want her people to see her in the lap of luxury and hate her for leading them into their crumbled defeat. Make sure you continue to get videos of her relaxing and enjoying her comfortable life here. We will broadcast them to every citizen of Lumina. We will put out this fake news so that every Lumina citizen hates her by the time we are finished."

* * *

In the quiet of her quarters, Quann waited. Each day that passed without a response from the Federation felt like an eternity. She refused to let despair take hold. She knew that the only way to succeed was to remain vigilant and patient and wait for another opportunity to work on the panel in her room.

One evening, as she sat by the window, gazing out at the star-filled sky watching a military celebration and parade, a soft beep alerted her to the hidden communication device. Her heart raced as she hurried to uncover it.

Despite being tired it was a perfect time to work on the device while the parade and celebration were going on. She frantically cleaned corroded wires and reconnected them to eroded terminals the best she could. With hours of tedious work she had no idea if she was making progress or not. With hope still echoing in her soul she closed the panel and covered it with the hanging tapestry.

*Hope is the compass that guides us
when the path is unclear.*

*Life's journey is often shrouded in uncertainty,
but hope serves as our compass,
pointing us toward the possibilities
that lie ahead despite our fear.
Even when the path is unclear to us,
hope provides the direction we need
to move with right purpose.*

Chapter 6

The Weight of the Crown

Princess Quann stood alone on a vast plain under a dark, stormy sky. The wind howled around her. She feels the weight of an invisible crown pressing down on her head. In confusion she looks down and sees that the vast plain is covered with the shadowy outlines of people; her beloved people of the Lumina Sector, looking up at her with expectation and hope in their eyes as they turn to silent shadows. Their sunken gazes are heavy with the weight of responsibility.

The scene shifts abruptly. Princess Quann finds herself in the grand throne room of the Lumina Sector. The room is dimly lit, and the walls seem to close in around her. She walks toward the throne, but each step feels like wading through thick grey water, slowing her down. As she approaches the throne, it begins to grow taller and more imposing, until it towers above her, casting a long dominent shadow. Her heart pounds as she realizes how small she feels in the face of this immense responsibility.

Then in a blink, the shadowy figures of her advisors, friends, and family appear, circling around her. They start to speak in unison, their voices echoing in her mind, questioning her ability to lead, protect, and guide her people. With her own hands around her throat she tries to speak, to assure everyone befor her that she is ready, but her voice fails her. The words are trapped in her throat. The more she struggles, the more the voices grow louder and more overwhelming.

The shadowy shifting scene morphes once more. Princess Quann is now standing at the edge of a tall, majestic waterfall. The water cascades down with a deafening roar. She can feel the mist on her face. Below her, the pool of water looks cool and inviting, but the height is dizzying. She hesitates, looking back at the throne room that has somehow followed her to the edge of the waterfall. The throne is still there, looming behind her, and she knows she must either jump into the unknown or be crushed by the weight of her future responsibilities.

Gathering all her courage, Princess Quann closes her eyes and leaps off the edge of the waterfall. For a brief moment, she feels nothing but the sensation of falling, as though she's lost control completely but then, she hits the cool water below, and the shock of it awakens her senses. As she sinks into the refreshing depths, the voices and the weight of the crown dissipate, leaving her feeling cleansed and renewed. She floats to the surface, realizing that the water has washed away her doubts, even if only temporarily.

Princess Quann wakes up in her quarters, her heart still racing from the dream. She sits up, staring out the window at the starry sky, contemplating what the dream meant. The fear is still there, but so is the resolve to face it, knowing that her future as queen is inevitable and that she can and must rise to the challenge.

**Hope remains the faithful friend
when all else fails.**

*In moments of gloom,
when everything seems to have abandoned us,
hope stays by our side.
It is the loyal companion that never wavers,
offering comfort and encouragement
when all other sources of strength have faltered.
Hope's presence is a testament
to its enduring power.*

Chapter 7

An Indomitable Spirit

As Virox's forces continued to tighten their grip on the galaxy, a tiny light of hope continued to flicker in Princess Quann's heart. Hours turned into days, days into weeks of hope beyond hope. Her quiet rebellion fueled by her commitment to the citizens of the Lumina Sector. Her untiring spirit fanned the flame of resistance. Her hope set the stage for a daring rescue. The Galactic Federation continued to hold its breath waiting for the right moment when the plans of the strength of the Galactic Federation Forces coincided with a moment when Virox's forces might be off guard. Patience was the Federations primary strategy.

The commanders of Virox's fleet were relentless in their pursuit of control. They fortified planets, hunted down rebels, and spread fear across the galaxy. But even in the face of such overwhelming odds, small pockets of resistance persisted. Inspired by the courage of Princess Quann, they fought back in whatever ways they could, refusing to be silenced.

* * *

Within the dimly lit command center of the Dominator, Chancellor Virox stood with his hands clasped behind his back, a satisfied smirk tugging at the corners of his lips. Before him, the vast holographic display of the galaxy flickered to life, casting an eerie glow across the room. Each sector that fell under his control lit up with a sinister red hue, a visual testament to his relentless conquest. One by one, entire star systems were engulfed by his expanding dominion, their defenses crumbling under the weight of his ruthless strategy. Virox's cold eyes traced the map, watching as his iron grip tightened around the galaxy, knowing that soon there would be no refuge left for those who dared oppose him. The galaxy, once a vibrant tapestry of diverse civilizations, was now being systematically consumed by the shadow of his empire.

"Victory is within our grasp," he mused, his voice a low growl, "The galaxy, including every sector of the Federation, will bow to my will, and those who oppose me will be crushed."

His confidence was unshakable, his obsession absolute. But even the most formidable tyrant could not foresee every twist of fate or the indomitable spirit of those who fought for freedom.

* * *

In the heart of the Federation, preparations for the rescue mission were underway. Kael Ventara, Riz Talon, and Mara Steeler, along with a team of elite support operatives, were readying themselves for the most dangerous mission of their lives. The consequences were significant but their tenacity was unbreakable.

Kael turned from the whiteboard and looked at his assembled team. He spoke with a voice filled with admiration, "On the surface our mission is simple, to rescue Princess Quann and bring her back safe and sound, but we all know this won't be a cake walk. Trust in your training, trust in each other, and we will succeed."

The team responded with nods of agreement, their faces set with willpower. They knew the risks, but they also knew what was at stake. The future of the galaxy depended on their success.

* * *

As the rescue mission launched, the Starfire sped towards Virox's stronghold. They were ready to face whatever challenges lay ahead, united in their mission to rescue Princess Quann and restore peace to the galaxy.

The endless expanse of space stretched out before them, a vast canvas of familiar stars twinkling in the darkness, each one a beacon calling them toward unknown horizons. These distant lights, once symbols of wonder and discovery, now held the promise of new challenges, uncharted worlds, and epic battles yet to be fought. The journey ahead was fraught with peril, the path littered with unseen threats and formidable enemies. Yet, as Kael Ventara gazed out at the starlit void, a steely resolve filled his chest. He and his team had faced impossible odds before, defying fate with courage and unity. This time would be no different. Together, they would carve their names into the annals of history once more, pushing beyond the limits of the known and into the realm of legend.

In the shadow of Virox's rule, the forces of oppression grew ever stronger. Yet, within the heart of his stronghold, Princess Quann's spirit remained unbroken. Her stolid rebellious nature and strategic mind set the stage for a daring escape, as the hope to maintain independence from fear of oppression continued to burn brightly, even in these most difficult of times.

*Hope is the seed that grows
even in the harshest soil.*

*Adversity tests us,
but it is in these harsh conditions
that hope takes root and flourishes.
Like a resilient plant, hope thrives
where other forces might wither.
It teaches us that progress is possible
even in the most challenging circumstances.*

Chapter 8

The Asteroid Field Chase

The dense, jagged rocks of the asteroid field loomed ahead, casting ominous shadows against the backdrop of the distant stars. The Starfire hurtled forward, engines roaring as Kael, Mara, and Riz braced themselves for the ambush they knew was coming. The asteroid field was a labyrinth of danger, with colossal rocks colliding and fragmenting, creating a constantly shifting maze.

Inside the cockpit, the tension could be read on everyone's furrowed brow. Kael's eyes were fixed on the controls, his grip tight. Mara's fingers danced over the weapons system, ready to unleash a barrage of laser fire. Riz was monitoring the shields, adjusting power levels to ensure they could withstand the impending onslaught.

"Hold on, team. We're going in hot. These asteroids are our only cover," Kael said, his voice steady despite the adrenaline coursing through his veins.

Mara glanced at the radar, "Virox's fighters are right on our tail, Kael. We've got to outmaneuver them or we're toast!"

Riz's hands moved quickly over the controls, "Redirecting all power to the shields. We need every bit of protection we can get in this rock storm."

Kael nodded. He was focused, "Good call, Riz. Mara, keep those weapons primed. We're going to need them."

"You got it. Just give me a clear shot," Mara replied, her eyes narrowing as she tracked the enemy fighters closing in.

The Starfire weaved through the asteroid field, Kael's hands moving across the panel of lit controls. Sharp turns and rolls helped them evade the enemy fire, but the asteroids around them exploded into debris as laser blasts from Virox's fighters narrowly missed their mark.

"Mara, how's it looking?" Kael asked, his voice tense.

Mara laughed, a note of defiance in her tone, "Good shot, trigger boy. That is not the first time you blasted an asteroid knowing the debris would smash up a fighter on your tail. They should teach that trick in fighter school and call it the 'Kael Asteroid Maneuver."

Kael smirked, his concentration unbroken, "Let's make it through this first. Then we can talk about naming maneuvers after me."

The radio crackled to life, Virox's cold voice cutting through the static, "Kael Ventara, you cannot escape. Surrender now and perhaps I'll show mercy."

Kael's jaw clenched, "Virox, you underestimate us. We're not going down without a fight."

Virox's laughter echoed through the comm-system, "Foolish bravery. You'll find the asteroid field less forgiving than I am."

"Got one! That's one less to worry about. How many more are there?" Mara shouted, her fingers flying over the weapons controls.

Riz checked the sensors, his face grim, "At least four more on our tail. Kael, we need to shake them off!"

"Hang on, I've got an idea. Riz, can you overload the thrusters for a short burst?" Kael asked, his mind racing.

"It'll be risky, but I can do it. Just say when," Riz replied, his hands poised over the controls.

"Now!" Kael commanded.

The Starfire suddenly surged forward into a horizontal thrust, accelerating at breakneck speed through a narrow gap that made them all crouch as if ducking through a narrow egress. Kael steered the ship sideways into the narrow gap between two colossal asteroids, the walls of rock mere inches from their hull. The enemy fighters struggled to keep up, two of them crashing into the asteroids and exploding into fiery wrecks.

"Yes! That's two more down!" Mara cheered, her eyes alight with triumph.

"We're not out of this yet. Riz, how are those shields holding?" Kael asked, his voice tight with urgency.

Riz grimaced, "They won't hold for long at this rate. We need to lose the last two fighters before we take any more hits."

"Mara, aim for the weak points on those ships. We need to take them out fast," Kael instructed, his tone commanding.

"On it!" Mara replied, her focus intense.

Virox's voice crackled over the comms again, frustration evident, "Ventara! You and your crew will pay for this insolence!"

Kael's voice was calm, defiant, "Maybe, Virox, but not today."

As the Starfire twisted and turned through the asteroid field, Mara unleashed a volley of precise shots, hitting the weak spots on the remaining enemy fighters. One by one, they erupted into flames, their debris scattering into the void.

Riz let out a relieved breath, "We did it! All clear, Kael."

Kael sighed in relief, "Nice shooting, Mara. Riz, great job on the shields. We're still in one piece thanks to you both."

"Hope, teamwork and a lick of luck, makes for success. If we keep up with close calls like this I might just regret coming along on this mission you bonehead." Mara said, a grin spreading across her face.

Kael smiled, feeling that old awareness of camaraderie, "Right. Now let's get out of this asteroid field and get back on track. We've still got a princess to save."

As the Starfire emerged from the treacherous asteroid field, the crew felt a their unity was as solid as ever. Their narrow escape had solidified their bond, preparing them for the challenges that lay ahead in their daring mission to rescue Princess Quann. The stars stretched out before them, each one a beacon of hope as they continued their journey through the galaxy.

**Hope sometimes reminds us that rest
is not the end, but a pause.**

In the ebb and flow of life, moments of rest
can feel like the end of our journey,
yet hope reframes these pauses
as essential interludes.
It teaches us that rest is not a sign of weakness
or defeat but a necessary part
of growth and renewal.
In rest, hope sees potential, not conclusion.

Chapter 9

Secrets of the Past

After narrowly escaping Chancellor Virox's deadly ambush in the asteroid field, the three warriors landed on the hidden planet of Elyria to make minor repairs to the Starfire before continuing their mission to rescue Princess Quann. This remote, serene world, blanketed in lush forests and surrounded by mist-shrouded mountains, is the home of an ancient martial arts order. Magnificent towering stone temples, worn by time, dot the landscape, exuding a tranquil sense of peace and wisdom.

As the crew walks through the tranquil forests of Elyria, the sound of rustling leaves and distant waterfalls creates a soothing atmosphere. They approach the largest temple, its grand archway welcoming them into a world of ancient wisdom. Inside, they are greeted by an elderly master named Master Elion.

Kael is in awe of the grand buildings, "This place is amazing. It's incredible. The peace here is almost tangible."

Mara nodded, "It's like stepping into another world, hundreds of years in the past. I can see why they chose this place for their order."

Riz adjusts his gear, "Let's hope these guys are friendly enough and can offer us a place to stay while I work on the Starfire. It might take days for me to fix all of the damage that we just received. We could all use a bit of clarity to unwind after what we've just been through."

As they enter the main hall, they are greeted by Master Elion, an elderly martial arts master with a serene presence and piercing eyes that seem to see into their very souls.

Master Elion bowed slightly, "Welcome, dear travelers."

Kael responded with a smile, "We seek a place to stay for two or three nights while we fix our starship. Our journey has been, well, to say it simply, it has been challenging. These are my navigator and mechanic, Mara and Riz, and I am Captain Kael Ventara. Just call me Kael."

Master Elion smiled kindly, "A place to rest you shall have, and perhaps you will find more than you seek. This main hall is called a "dojo". We will find you a room in a smaller building that is just beyond. For now I will arrange for some refreshments for you. Kael Ventara, I know your family name well. We have much to talk about. I sense that you already feel a connection within you to this place. Please, walk with me."

Kael follows Master Elion deeper into the dojo, while the other two are shown to a serene courtyard to rest.

Master Elion led Kael through a garden, "This place holds many secrets, Kael. I feel the burden you carry, but also a light within you. Tell me, what do you know of your family?"

Kael paused thoughtfully, "Not much. My mother passed away when I was young, and my father never spoke of her family but he gave me her family name to honour her. All I have are fragments of memories and a sense of something more. Why do you ask?"

Master Elion nodded with a slight bow, "I believe that your mother's father's name was Rohen Ventara. He was a revered master of our order and one of my teachers. We called him Master Ventara. He was a great Odika Master and had a deep connection to the Divine. I see that same undeveloped potential in you, Kael, it is deep in your DNA."

Kael looked surprised, "My grandfather was a great Odika Master? My mother taught me some martial arts and different forms of meditation when I was young but I never had any formal training."

Master Elion smiled, "Come, sit with me. Close your eyes and breathe. Let go of your fears and doubts. The answers lie within. You can release what is already part of your foundation, of your being."

Kael sits cross-legged beside Master Elion, closing his eyes and focusing on his breath. As he meditates in a formal way for the first time, he feels warmth spreading through his body, a connection to something greater than he has ever felt.

Kael speaks softly, "It is interesting. I can feel it. I can feel something. A presence, a strength that I have felt before but have never fully understood."

Master Elion speaks encouragingly, "Kael, that is the legacy of your grandfather that you are feeling. As I said, it is part of your DNA. The Odika techniques he mastered have been taught for centuries and are deep within you. Trust in them. Let the Divine guide you and you will feel the guidance in many different ways. I feel a sense of despair in you but it is clocked in hope. Your Grandfather taught that hope is never lost. There are always unexplored possibilities. Lack of hope simply means lack of faith and lack of imagination."

Kael, in an almost whisper told the story about intuitively finding Riz and Mara for the mission, "I don't want to sound weird or anything but it was like I was led to the exact place where they would be."

Master Elion smiled, "That is what happens to each of us when we trust and allow ourselves to be open and led by the divine. Everyone has this ability. Everyone. You are not one of the 'chosen' as some choose to believe but you are one of the 'open'. Open because of how the teachings were passed from your grandfather to your mother and to you, simply in subtle ways." Master Elion smiled and said softly, "Enough talking for now, just sit and be calm and listen. Focus on the calm that fills every moment, the calm that fills all space, the calm that is All-in-all."

Kael delves deeper into his meditation, sensing the flow of calm around and within him. Minutes turn to hours and all sense of time stopped. Memories of his mother and glimpses of his grandfather began to surface, filling him with a profound sense of divine purpose and clarity.

Kael opened his eyes, "I feel it, Master Elion. I understand something more now. This connection. It has always been a part of me."

Master Elion nodded, "Indeed. It is part of everyone. Use this newfound strength wisely, Kael. It will aid you in the challenges ahead. Remember, true power comes from within. It is through peace that you will find your greatest strength."

Kael stands, feeling a deeper connection to his past. He bows to Master Elion, gratitude evident in his eyes, "Thank you, Master Elion. I won't forget this. I will honour my grandfather's legacy."

Master Elion smiled, "Go forth with wisdom and courage, Kael Ventara. The Divine is always with you, always."

Kael returns to his comrades, his newfound clarity and strength evident. The connection between the crew is strengthened as they prepare for the next stage of their mission, knowing that they carry not only their own hopes but the legacy of those who came before them.

They enjoy a simple dinner with some Odika students and teachers. The meal was accompanied by calm, meditative music. The night was restful, the serene atmosphere helping them to unwind. Riz worked diligently on the Starfire, completing all necessary repairs in two days. The crew waked rested and rejuvenated, ready for the next phase of their journey of heading to Chancellor Virox's Royal Palace. All they need now are the final orders from Federation Headquarters. Will the rest of the team be ready with exit support ships? Is everyone on the same page with an in and out schedule?

If there was one thing that Kael had learned in the last two days, it was to trust in the Divine. Demanding answers or explanations from anyone was futile and only led to frustration. Instead, he had to place his faith in the resilience of hope and the expectation of good. It was a profound lesson in patience and belief, understanding that sometimes the most powerful force was the quiet confidence that everything would unfold as it should. The Divine, with its mysterious ways, provided a sense of peace and assurance that surpassed any immediate answers or clear-cut paths.

Hope is the power of possibilities
when all seems lost.

When the world narrows
and choices seem to vanish,
hope expands the mind's horizon.
Hope transforms impossibility into opportunity,
reminding us that even in the bleakest moments,
there's a chance to rewrite the future.
Hope is the alchemy that turns despair into the
prospect that all will be well.

Chapter 10
The Holographic Message Received

Princess Quann stood on the high balcony of her luxurious suite in Chancellor Virox's Royal Palace, her eyes scanning the sprawling city below. The view was breathtaking with tall buildings and mountains in the distance but there was a conspicuous absence of nature. There were no trees or grass, no paths leading through fountain adorned parks. For the first time, she realized there were no birds or animals, not even a dog or cat. The sunrise was beautiful but it did little to ease her mind. Some days it was like time stood still. Mesmerised by her captive stillness she gazed at the constant quietude and allowed her mind to flicker into her childhood. As an only child she remembered the calm stillness in the courtyard of her Royal Palace that was seldom used.

Now on the Virox Palace balcony she gazed at her childhood. She remembered the calm stillness in the courtyard where she played and skipped with visiting friends. The quiet garden of Princess Quann's childhood was a mental sanctuary, a place where time seemed to pause, allowing her to reflect amidst the rustling leaves of the past and the gentle hum of nature. Her childhood garden was a masterpiece of tranquility, with pathways lined by fragrant blossoms and ancient trees offering shaded canopies. Birds sang softly from their hidden perches, and a delicate fountain trickled, its water sparkling in the dappled sunlight.

Quann's memories flooded over her as she remembered fencing lessons with Maître Armand Dufresne. Lesson after lesson after warm-ups, she was expected to practice footwork drills and blade exercises. Her favorite part of daily exercises was practicing attack and defense techniques, followed by controlled sparring, and concluding with feedback and cool-down stretches. Over the years of lessons she gained poise, confidence and self-reliance.

She would often sit by the rose-covered trellis, breathing in the sweet perfume, letting the memories of her carefree youth wash over her. This garden of her youth, with its serene beauty, was a reflection of her inner strength and the quiet resilience she grew within. Little did she know that this foundation of life would be the elements of her being that she would rely on in her capture.

She refused to give in to despair, her defiant spirit and tactical mind remained sharp. She counted on being rescued by the Federation, and she was determined to help make it happen if she possibly could.

Days passed. It had been many days since she had found the comm-panel behind the heavy tapestry. She continued to spent fleeting moments tinkering with it, fearful of being caught. The cameras in the room didn't point directly at the comm-panel, but she couldn't risk being out of sight for too long.

One afternoon, as she worked on the panel, a guard brought her lunch and almost caught her. She managed to divert his attention just in time. With her heart pounding in her chest she managed to divert his attention with a smile, asking him if his family was happy and well. After many hours of painstaking effort, she was confident that she could finally send a message.

Princess Quann kept track of the times when it was safe to make an attempt. Finally, when she felt it was safe, she sent out a desperate plea: "Attention, Galactic Federation Forces, this is Princess Quann. I am being held captive in Chancellor Virox's Royal Palace on the 27th floor. The Virox forces are getting ready for a major attack on the Federation. Be prepared."

Meanwhile, in the heart of Virox's stronghold, a guard rushed into the grand chamber where Chancellor Virox sat, "Chancellor, we have intercepted a message that was sent from Princess Quann's suite where she is being held," the guard reported, his voice trembling with fear that retribution would be inflicted on him.

Virox's eyes narrowed, "She sent a message from her quarters? How is that possible? I want an explanation. Someone will pay for allowing this to happen. Increase the security around her. Move her to a prison cell. Let's see how defiant she remains in less comfortable surroundings."

* * *

The dark, oppressive confines of Princess Quann's new cell were suffocating. The dimly lit room had only one small, barred window offering a glimpse of sky between tall buildings. Despite the dire situation, Quann's attitude did not falter. She spent more and more time in her peaceful youth, swimming in the private lake with her nanny. She rowed over its still waters and jogged its shaded paths.

Her peaceful nature allowed her to chat and make friends with a young guard named Arin. She asked him questions about his family and life outside of serving Chancellor Virox. Within very few days she gained his trust. Was it because she was a princess or because she was a pretty young woman? Princess Quann asked simple questions about his personal life trying to gain more sympathetic support. She slowly wormed her way into his confidence. She took the risk of asking a favour that might backfire on both of them but the risk was worth taking and it did pay off.

One night, Arin approached her cell, glancing around nervously, "Princess, I've brought the comm-devise that you asked for. But we must be quick. Other guards will pass by here soon. I can't be caught talking with you."

Princess Quann slipped a ring off of her hand and gave it to Arin, "Thank you, Arin. This will ensure your family's safety. If you are smart and get a good price for the ring it will be more than enough. It has been in my family for hundreds of years. Now, let's get this message sent before someone comes along."

Arin activated the small communication device that was no larger than his baby finger, "What do you need me to do now?"

Princess Quann inserted a micro data chip into the device and explained, "This chip contains the coordinates of Virox's Royal Palace, details of the cells, cameras and details of his latest plans. We need to send it to the Federation immediately. With this info you can rest assured that you have saved hundreds, if not thousands of lives. You are a true hero Arin. If this message is received successfully I will hunt for you and make sure you are rescued and rewarded."

Arin worked quickly, his hands shaking slightly as he prepared to send the message. The device flickered silently casting a couple of red lights onto the ceiling of the cell.

"The device is ready, Princess," Arin said nervously.

"Good. Now, transmit the message," Quann instructed, her voice purposeful.

The holographic image of Princess Quann shimmered to life and was flawlessly sent exactly as Private Arin recorded it. At long last the message was sent successfully but hope beyond hope, no one knew if it would be received by the Federation. If received by the right people, its impact would be immense. Arin deactivated the device and quickly concealed it.

With fondness burning in his eyes, he handed Princess Quann the ring back, "I can't take this as payment, dear Princess. Freedom one day for my children is the only payment that is needed. If I have an opportunity I will send the message again just to make sure it gets out of this hell hole. Stay strong, Princess."

Arin disappeared down a dark corridor and was never seen again.

Princess Quann, whispered under her breath, "Thank you, Arin. May the stars guide you always."

* * *

At the Galactic Federation Headquarters, officers monitored various communications. Suddenly, an urgent alert sounded, "Ambassador Zane, we have an incoming holographic message. It's marked with Princess Quann's identification code," the Communications Officer announced.

Ambassador Zane rushed over, "Patch it through immediately."

The holographic image of Princess Quann flickered to life, "This is Princess Quann. I am being held in Virox's stronghold on the planet Zygara. I have been moved to a prison cell eight floors below ground. The attached document includes a floor plan of the building with security cameras. Chancellor Virox plans to launch a major offensive against the Federation sometime soon. You must be ready and act quickly. Over."

The message ended abruptly. Ambassador Zane turned to his officers, his face set with grit, "We need to act fast. Has anyone heard from Captain Ventara? The last we heard he narrowly survived a skirmish with a Virox patrol. They are on their way to the Virox Royal Palace. The last intel we sent them was that Princess Quann was held captive on the 27th floor. We have to update them asap. Send this message and all of the data. They will need every bit of the information. For all we know, they are hovering in the asteroid field right now waiting for details and our instructions."

Hope is the expectation of good.

Hope believes in the possibility of change,
nurturing the seeds
of personal and collective evolution.
It drives us to improve,
to become more than we are today.
With hope, the expectation of good
leads to growth
and becomes not just a wish,
but an inevitable result.

Chapter 11

Asteroid Fields
are a Good Place to Hide

The cockpit of the Starfire hummed with activity as the crew strapped in. The engines roared to life, and the ship lifted off, accelerating into the vast expanse of space.

Kael piloted the ship with a focused intensity, "Everyone ready for hyperspace?

Mara smirked, "Always ready for whatever you throw at us, Captain."

Riz grinned, "Let's show Virox what we're made of."

* * *

The Starfire sped through hyperspace leaving streams of light in their wake. The crew went over their plan one last time, the ship's interior hummed with the energy of eagerness.

Kael addressed the crew, "We still have to receive the final orders from HQ. I have no idea when that will be. If we get there before them, we will hide out in the Alarin Asteroid Field. The metallic structure of the asteroids will shield our presence.

* * *

Hours of silently hiding in the asteroid field led to more hours and more hours of tedious boredom. Finally, the comm-system came alive. Riz jumped to hit the audio button. The Anxious voice of Ambassador Zane filled the cockpit telling that Princess Quann had been moved from the Royal Palace to a holding cell. Mara scanned through the many files the Princess Quann included in the transmission. Mara cheered with joy, "This is amazing, Princess Quann has not only given us a map of where to find her but a schematic of the electric panels, comm-panels, camera panels and more. She has turned this rescue mission into a walk in the park."

Kael continued reading the documents that included the support teams´ arrival time, "It looks like we still have a couple more hours to sit and wait before the support ship arrives. Once they are hidden in the asteroid field with us, we will be given the go ahead to make our way in."

The next couple of hours dragged on for ever.

"Support Team to Captain Ventara, come in please."

Kael slapped his chair, "Finally you have arrived. Where have you been? No, don't answer that! We don't have enough time. Our window of opportunity for heading in during this day shift is closing. We have to move quickly or we have to wait for another shift rotation and we don't want to do that. If you don't have anything new to tell us, we are heading in. Just be ready with your fingers on the trigger. It is likely we will need your support when we come flying out of there with Princess Quann."

* * *

"Alright, listen up," Kael addressed the crew, "Don't forget that we are going in with no cloak and dagger and no shields up. We want them to see us. We want them to think we are just a routine ship coming in for drop off and pick up. I will have my comm-panel open and wait for them to give us permission to land. We want the guard to think our arrival is just a normal routine visit. Riz, you'll handle their cameras and alarms as soon as we're past the guards. Mara, your job is to guide us through the corridors and tunnels inside the building."

Mara nodded energetically, "We've been over this a hundred times. Once we are inside we need to be quick and precise. Ok, we got it." With a sense of sarcasm Mara smirked, "I think you must be hyper nervous. You forgot to mention one more time that we need to get in and out fast – no room for mistakes."

Riz smiled at Mara but spoke quickly, "I'll keep the ship ready for a quick getaway. My remote control will get the Starfire fired up with ramp down as we approach the ship. As soon as you give me the signal, we will be catapulted into outer space before you can say space monkey. We're going in and out fast."

* * *

The planet Zygara loomed ahead, its darkened surface reflecting the ominous threat it held. The Starfire dropped out of hyperspace, its sleek form cutting through the darkness of space towards the docking bay and the waiting guards.

Kael activated the comm-system on an open channel, "Come in Virox docking bay. This is captain Ventara of the starship Starfire. We are approaching your landing zone and are asking permission to land. Over."

The Virox docking bay replied, "This is Virox Landing Bay F5, Officer Paylen. Please state your purpose for landing, who you are expecting to see and how long you will be disembarked. Over."

Mara crossed her fingers and readied her weapons, "We're coming, Princess Quann. Just hold on a little longer."

Kael cleared his throat, "Come in Virox Landing Bay, I don't know who I am supposed to report to but we are Rebel bounty hunters under orders from Chancellor Virox. We were directed here to collect our payment by reporting here in person.

Maybe you can point us in the right direction. All we want is our cashola, buddy, and we will be on our way. We will be in and out in a flash. We won't even turn off our engines, that is how fast we will be. Over."

* * *

The docking bay was shrouded in an eerie silence with very little activity. Kael, Mara, and Riz wore the rugged attire of bounty hunters, complete with weapons on their hips and over their shoulders. They clenched their forged identification. The towering structure of the fortress loomed a short distance away casting an ominous pall over the entire area. Menacing black steel buildings loomed in the distance with heavily armed guards marching in formation from one building to another.

Kael adjusted his gear, his eyes scanning the team, "Remember, we're bounty hunters here for a job. Stick to the strategy, and we'll be in and out before they know it."

Mara checked her blaster, her expression grave, "Got it. Let's hope these disguises hold up."

Riz nodded, "I've got the security codes ready. All we need is permission to land and we are in action."

The docking guard spoke, "Starfire, give me a minute, I am checking with dispatch to see if you are at the right docking bay. You might have to go to F7. Let me check. Over."

A few nervous minutes passed. The three sat as patiently as possible.

In a gruff tone, Kael grumbled, "Hey buddy, we're here just to collect our reward. Let us dock and I will show you our papers. Over."

The docking guard spoke, "Starfire, pull into V29, turn off your engines and report to me at F5. It is clearly marked past hanger B. Over and out."

The trio approached the main entrance at F5. They walked with the confidence of seasoned bounty hunters. The checkpoint was guarded by imposing sentries, their faces obscured by dark helmets and face shields. Kael stepped forward, presenting their forged credentials with a confident swagger.

The guard was skeptical, his voice a low growl, "State your business."

Kael spoke up, "Like I said we are here to collect our payment from Chancellor Virox. We were supposed to report to some purser guy who handles the money. He's got a log of credits for us. That is all we want and then we will leave as fast as possible."

The guard eyed them suspiciously, his gaze lingering on their weapons, "This is all out of the ordinary. Why don't you have an appointment authorization number? Or at least a demand of payment invoice. Wait here."

As the guard verified their credentials, the team stood tense but outwardly calm. After a few moments, the guard stamped their paper work and waved them through, "Report to the Purser in room 1098. Blue door. Follow the yellow line and turn left. He will be waiting for you. You're clear. Don't go off the yellow line and don't stop to talk to anyone, don't cause any trouble. Just get in and out and make it quick. We have enough on our plates today. Alarms have been going on and off all day."

Kael nodded, "We won't be any trouble. Just here for the credits. I promise, we will be in and out before you know it."

Inside the fortress, the corridors were dimly lit and patrolled by guards and surveillance drones. The team moved stealthily, avoiding detection with practiced ease.

Mara whispered, "Next junction, we need to take the left. The security hub is that way."

Riz whispered in reply, "Got it. I'll disable the cameras once we're in."

They navigated the narrow corridors, using shadows and alcoves to evade patrols. They reached the security hub, a small room filled with monitors and controls.

In a rushed voice, Kael replied to Riz, "You're up. Disable the cameras and loop the footage."

Riz worked quickly, his fingers dancing over the keyboard. The monitors flickered, and the camera feeds froze on empty corridors.

Riz murmured quickly, "Done. We've got a small window. Let's go."

Deeper into the fortress, the corridors became more heavily guarded. The team encountered a group of soldiers and quickly ducked into a side room.

Mara listened intently, "They're coming this way. We need a distraction."

Kael spotted a maintenance panel, "I've got an idea. Mara, give me a hand."

They pried open the panel, causing a short circuit that set off a series of alarms and lights.

A soldier rushed past, "What the hell? Check it out! The alarms have been going on and off all day. I am getting tired of this."

As the soldiers moved towards the disturbance, the team slipped out and continued their infiltration.

Near the central holding cells, the air was tense, and the sense of danger was palpable. The team moved cautiously, their goal within reach.

Kael whispered, "According to the schematics, Princess Quann's cell should be just ahead."

* * *

The rescue team made their way with precision through the complicated labyrinth of corridors that led to cell block "D". Mara chimed in, "I am sure glad that Virox had Princess Quann moved to this cell block. It would have been a lot harder to get into the Royal Palace."

Kael and Mara took out guards silently, ensuring their path remained clear. Riz monitored their progress from a comm-tablet that confirmed their every move. The intel that Princess Quann provided was accurate right down to the number of light fixtures on the ceiling and a broom closet with a maintenance number painted in blue.

As they neared Princess Quann's cell, Kael signaled for Mara to take position, "We're almost there. Be ready."

Mara nodded, her weapon at the ready. They reached the cell door, and Kael quickly disabled the lock. The door swung open, revealing Princess Quann standing resolutely.

"Princess Quann, we're here to rescue you," Kael said, stepping inside.

Princess Quann's eyes lit up with gratitude, "Thank you. Thank you. I knew you would come."

* * *

The team moved swiftly, guiding Princess Quann through the corridors towards the extraction point. Their progress was steady, but the alarm was soon raised. Guards flooded the corridors, and the team engaged in a fierce firefight.

Kael and Mara provided cover as they made their way to the exit. Riz coordinated their extraction, ensuring the Starfire was ready for a quick getaway.

"Hold the line!" Kael shouted, firing at the approaching guards.

"We're almost there!" Mara replied, her shots precise and lethal.

Princess Quann stayed close, her heart pounding with adrenaline. They burst through the final door, the Starfire waiting for them.

* * *

The crew of the Starfire fought their way back to the ship, determination fueling their every move. They boarded quickly. Riz was the first one on, firing up the engines before he even set foot on the ramp. The ramp was rising to close as Mara stepped on board. Kael shouted to blast off as it lifted from the concrete platform leaving the stronghold behind.

Kael turned to Princess Quann, "We're not out of danger yet but we have a support team ready and waiting."

"Captain Ventara of the StarFire to GFF Support Team. We have Princess Quann and we are already in flight. Be ready with support, we have Virox fighters hot on our tail. Over."

"GFF Support here, we have you on our scanners and are ready for you. Just head on past us. We will take care of the Virox fighters. They are no match for us. Over and out."

The Starfire maneuvered through space, avoiding enemy fire. The crew worked seamlessly, their bond evident in every action.

"We've got incoming!" Mara warned, firing at the pursuing ships.

"Hold on tight," Riz said, pushing the Starfire to its limits.

* * *

Finally, the ship broke free of the enemy's grasp, entering the safety of hyperspace. The crew breathed a collective sigh of relief, their mission a success.

Princess Quann looked at her rescuers, gratitude and determination shining in her eyes, "Thank you all. The Galactic Federation and The Lumina Sector owe you a great debt."

Kael smiled, "We couldn't have done it without you and the intel that you sent us."

Princess Quann reached across the command chairs and squeezed his hand, lingering longer than expected, "Thank you" were her only words."

Kael smiled and pulled his hand away, "Princess, now let's get you home."

As the Starfire sped towards Federation space, the crew knew their journey was far from over. But for now, they had achieved a great victory, one that would inspire people across the galaxy.

**Hope is the anchor that holds us steady
even in the strongest storm.**

*Life's storms are inevitable,
but hope provides stability.
Like an anchor, it grounds us,
preventing us from drifting into despair.
No matter how fierce the winds
or how rough the seas,
hope keeps us secure,
allowing us to weather any tempest.*

Chapter 12

Decrypted into Hope

Princess Quann was safe and out of the clutches of Chancellor Virox, but the threat to the demise of the Federation still loomed. As the team regrouped and prepared for their next move, their bond grew stronger, and their resolve became unbreakable. The infiltration and rescue were just the beginning; the battle for the galaxy's freedom from Virox was far from over.

* * *

Ambassador Zane stood in the Federation War Room watching the red dot that represented the Starfire enter the safety of hyperspace after the rescue. With the stress of the rescue melting from his face, he was relieved that Kael and his team were already on their way home to the Federation Headquarters. His mind could now turn to hope beyond hope, the next unexpected phase of their operation, "We need to ensure the safety of Princess Quann and prepare for Virox's retaliation. Inform all sectors to be on high alert," he ordered.

"Yes, Ambassador," the communications officer replied, "We'll mobilize additional fleets to secure our borders and protect key installations."

Ambassador Zane nodded his ok but added, "Send a full fleet of ships to rendezvous with the Starfire as soon as possible. I want Princess Quann off of the Starfire and on our lead ship. We have to protect her with everything we have." His thoughts instantly flipped to the strategies needed to counter Virox's plans. Everyone knew that the battle was far from over, and that every decision made now could determine the fate of the galaxy.

* * *

Back on the Starfire, the crew were in high spirits, but the weight of the future of the Federation still lingered. Kael got everyone's attention, "Alright. We've got Princess Quann safe," He points with a smile to Princess Quann, "but now we have to decide if we should simply deliver her to Federation Headquarters as we are expected to do, or should we see what harm we can do to Virox and his forces before we head home?"

Mara nodded, her expression serious, "Here we go again. One more opportunity to look death square in the face. Don't forget that I signed on to rescue a pretty little princess not to save the bloody universe. I am all for doing damage to Virox but we need a plan. We just risked our life and now we are thinking about doing it again without any support from the Federation. What's our next move, Kael?"

Kael looked around the room, seeing true grit in his crew's eyes, "We need to analyze the data that Princess Quann risked her life to get. It's crucial we understand Virox's plans and relay this information to the Federation before we do anything. Princess Quann, you are stuck with us for now. What do you think about this? Do we rendezvous with the Federation ships and pass you over into safety or are you coming with us to the underground to see what damage we can do?

The Freedom Alliance Fighters (FAF) base is about three light hours away."

* * *

Princess Quann handed over the data chip to Riz, her expression one of fierce resolve, "The data on the chip has a ton of info but I am sure that Chancellor Virox is going to change all of the codes, schedules and missions within a day or day and a half so, if we are going to do anything against Chancellor Virox, we have to do it now. At least within this day. The chip contains everything I could gather about Virox's plans. We need to act quickly."

Riz nodded, "We'll get this to Ambassador Zane immediately. I'll make sure it is encrypted. We don't want to tip our hand to Virox."

Kael turned to Mara, "The two of you do your magic and get us in contact with Federation Command via hyper-link. They need to know where we are, what we know and what are our plans. Send Princess Quann's files. We need to know for sure that they have everything we have."

Mara quickly set up the communication link and nodded to Kael to go ahead, "Ambassador Zane, for the moment this will be a one-way conversation until we get closer to Federation Headquarters. This is Captain Ventara. As you know, we've secured Princess Quann and are analysing the data she secured. You might already have it but the attached file is everything that we have. We are trying to break the encryption as we speak. We are heading to an undisclosed coordinate to meet up with members of the Freedom Alliance Fighters – the FAF to see what damage we can do to Virox and his plans."

* * *

Mara shrieked with hands above her head, "Kael, get this, we did it! We broke the encryption of the file! We can see everything! Every file, the location of every outpost, how many ships and more. We can see everything. Way to go, Princess Quann! What you gave us is worth way more than you could have imagined." Mara laughed, "This Data is so valuable that it was worth you getting captured just so you could gather the intelligence. Boy is Virox ever going to be pissed off when he figures out that his plan to capture you turned around like a sand lizard and bit him in the face."

With two thumbs up, Kael smiled, "Way to go you two. I had every confidence in you. Send it to me in the conference room so the four of us can go over it. Princess Quann, I assume you will want to be in on this. After you have sent it to me you can re-encrypt it with Federation codes and send it to the Federation Headquarters. Ambassador Zane and General Thorne will be thrilled. Send it to the FAF – make sure it is encrypted. Even though they are the underground, they cracked that encryption a long time ago but the Federation doesn't know yet. Both Commander Peddler and Commander Vela will want to see this as soon as possible before we arrive. We are still hours away. It will give them time to analyze the data before we arrive. All of them will want to get their hands on it ASAP."

**Hope will always strengthen us
if we are too weary to walk.**

When exhaustion weighs heavy on our spirit,
hope becomes
the quiet source of renewed strength.
It doesn't always demand grand gestures;
instead,
it infuses us with the energy to continue.

Chapter 13

The Icy Refuge

After their daring escape from Virox's fortress, the crew of the Starfire sought refuge on the icy planet of Glacius. This foreboding planet was a harsh, frozen landscape, the perfect cover for the rebel base of operations. Its home base was hidden deep within an ice cave camouflaged in the steep cliffs of a frozen mountain.

Kael, navigating through the high winds of a storm. Glancing at the instrument panel he shouted, "We're almost there. Keep an eye out for the signal beacon."

Riz checked the controls and steadied his nerves, "Hang tight, everyone. This is going to be a bumpy almost blind landing."

Mara, scanning the sensors, pointed at the screen, "I see it! Adjust course to heading 245. The entrance to the base should be in that ice canyon." They spotted the hidden entrance to the rebel base, concealed within a massive ice wall.

The Starfire descended through the blizzard of treacherous winds, navigating limited visibility. The crew could feel the ship shudder as it fought against the elements. The engines of the Starfire hummed steadily as the crew braced the bumpy descent onto a short icy runway. Despite the harsh conditions, Kael's expert piloting kept them on course.

From the cockpit, the crew could see the desolate, frozen world with towering ice peaks and swirling snowstorms.

As Kael, Mara, Riz, and Princess Quann disembarked, they were greeted by fellow rebels, old allies, and new faces alike. Here, they regrouped, tended to their wounds, and planned their next move against Virox's tyranny. The frigid environment served as both a challenge and a shield, testing their endurance as they prepared for the next phase of their mission.

Commander Vela, a tall woman with a stern expression softened by a welcoming smile, approached, "Welcome to Glacius. I'm Commander Vela. We've been expecting you."

Kael shook Vela's hand firmly, "Thank you, Commander. We could use a safe haven right now."

Commander Vela nodded, "You'll find it here. Follow me. Commander Peddler warned me that you might be dropping in for a bit of a social call. I am glad you all arrived in one piece. Your motto of – One impossible mission at a time has never let you down. Peddler told me about your motto." Commander Vela laughed, "Someone in our group was so impressed with it that they wrote it on the wall of the bathroom stall."

Kael chuckled, "I wish it was just a social call. I assume that you received the encrypted file that we sent. Once we all understand what is in those files, I hope we will be making a bit of a social call on Chancellor Virox."

As they followed Commander Vela into the base, the crew marvelled at the ingenuity of the rebels. The base was a network of tunnels and chambers carved into the ice, illuminated by a combination of natural light filtering through the ice and advantageously placed lights. The temperature inside was slightly warmer, but still cold enough to see their breath.

* * *

Inside the rebel base, the crew was led to a warmer central ice cave that had corridors to housing, recreation and a large meeting room where a large holographic map of the galaxy was displayed. Everyone started to peel off their harsh weather shells. The room was bustling with activity, as rebels analised data and discussed strategies. The atmosphere was less tense as everyone started to warm up and were served a hot beverage.

Riz, with a perplexed look on his face leaned forward and said, "I am sorry if I am way off topic here but where is all of the heat coming from? What is your energy source to run all of this equipment? It is amazing."

Commander Vela laughed, "Usually people just take it all for granted and don't ask but Sargent Miles will give you a tour after our meeting but to give you a quick answer, it is all powered by water. Ice is water so we have plenty of fuel. To dumb it down into a high school chemistry lesson, as you know water itself cannot be used directly as a combustion fuel, but it can be a source of hydrogen, which is a powerful fuel. Through a process called electrolysis, water, as you know is, H_2O. It is split into hydrogen H_2 and oxygen O_2 gases using an electric current. The hydrogen gas can then be used as a fuel in combustion engines or fuel cells. The oxygen we pump throughout the habitat so we can breathe. It is a simple as that. When hydrogen burns or reacts in a fuel cell, it combines with oxygen, producing energy and water vapor as the only byproduct. Pretty cool. This makes hydrogen a clean energy source, with water being both the starting point and the end product of the process. Sargent Miles will give you a tour and a deeper statistical description of how much heat, water and electricity we get but basically this entire habitat was melted for fuel."

Riz was excited and said, "Yes, I am interested to know more but I guess we had better get down to business first."

Vela pointed to the map, "We've been monitoring Virox's movements for months now. His forces are spreading thin, but he still holds significant power. We need to strike strategically."

Princess Quann, her thick cloak still draped over her shoulders, stepped forward with a determined glint in her eyes. "During our escape, we managed to gather crucial intelligence," she began, her voice carrying the weight of what they had uncovered. "This isn't just any information—we've pinpointed the exact chink in his armor, the place where he's most vulnerable."

She paused, letting the gravity of her words sink in, her gaze steady and unyielding. "He's not invincible, not by a long shot. We have the knowledge that can turn the tide of this war. It's time to strike where it hurts the most, to take advantage of the weakness he thought was hidden."

Her voice grew firmer, charged with the resolve of someone who had seen the darkness up close but refused to be cowed by it. "We're not just fighting to survive anymore. We're fighting to win. And with this intel, we have the upper hand."

Kael rubbed his chin thoughtfully, "But we need more than just information. We need allies, resources, and a solid plan."

Mara leaned in, her eyes sharp, "And we need to be prepared for anything. Virox won't go down without a fight."

Commander Vela nodded, "Agreed. Let's review the data you've collected and see how we can use it to our advantage."

The crew spent the next few hours in intense discussions, analysing the information Princess Quann had secured. The data revealed the locations of Virox's supply depots, troop movements, and even potential weaknesses in his defences. It was a treasure trove of information, but they needed to act quickly before Virox could change his plans.

* * *

After the long meeting, in the medical bay, the crew took turns getting treated for their injuries. The bay was a modest setup, but the medics were skilled and efficient. Princess Quann sat on a cot, wincing as a medic bandaged her arm. This was not the first wound that she had received in battle.

The medic, gentle but firm, spoke softly, "You're lucky you made it out. We've lost many good people to Virox."

Princess Quann's eyes hardened, "We won't lose anyone else if I have anything to say about it. We are hoping that the intel that we gathered will help to save lives."

Nearby, Kael sat on another cot, being treated for a wound on his side, "We're going to need everyone's help. The Federation, the rebels, anyone willing to stand against Virox."

The medic finished up and gave a nod, "You'll find plenty of willing souls here. Just give them some level of hope, even if it is hope beyond hope." He chuckled, "Hope is each of our middle names."

As the crew recuperated, they shared stories of their journey and the people they had lost along the way. The camaraderie among them grew stronger, fortified by their shared purpose and determination.

* * *

Later, in a large communal hall, the crew and rebels gathered for a meal. The hall was filled with long tables and benches, and the atmosphere was lively despite the underlying tension. The rebels were a diverse group, from many different planets and moons. They were seasoned fighters and fresh recruits, all united by their desire to overthrow Virox and his tyrannical empire. There was no other goal, no other motive; there was no other objective or purpose in any of the strategies that were executed.

Amongst the whirlwind of enthusiasm Kael contemplated and admired the singular non-political purpose that motivated the Freedom Alliance Fighters – the fight against tyranny. His mind flew back to all of the politically motivated wars that he as a Galactic Federation Forces warrior had be a pawn in. The FAF was a group that he finally felt an affinity for.

Riz stood up, raising a glass, "To freedom, and to the end of Virox's tyranny!"

The rebels cheered in unison, "To freedom!"

Vela stood, addressing the group with a commanding presence, "We've all suffered under Virox's rule. But together, we can bring about his downfall. Our strength is in our unity."

Kael, standing beside Vela, added his voice, "We have a plan, and we have the courage to see it through. Let's make every sacrifice count."

The room erupted into cheers and applause. Unity and resolve reverberated from person to person.

Hope doesn't wait for the perfect moment;
it seizes the occasion.

Hope doesn't sit idly by,
waiting for circumstances to align.
Instead, it takes initiative,
and recognizes opportunities where none existed.
Hope is the force that transforms the present,
making what seems impossible today
possible tomorrow.

Chapter 14

Hope's Expectation of Success

Later that night, in the dimly lit war room, Kael, Mara, Riz, Princess Quann, and Commander Vela gathered around the holographic map that shimmered with an eerie blue light over the projector. The atmosphere was thick with tension, each person acutely aware of the stakes. The room was quiet, the only sound was the low hum of the projector, punctuated by the occasional beep of the control panels lining the walls.

Commander Vela leaned in, her finger tracing a path across the map before pausing at a key location. "Virox's main supply depot is here," she stated, her voice filled with a sense of urgency. "A successful raid on this location would cripple his operations and bring Chancellor Virox to his knees."

Kael, his expression hardened with resolve, nodded in agreement. "Agreed. We need to hit him where it hurts the most, but we'll need more precise intel to time this perfectly."

Mara, her brow furrowed in thought, spoke up. "We could tap into our old contacts in the Federation. They might have the resources and information we need to pull this off."

Princess Quann, her voice steady yet firm, added, "I'll reach out to our allies immediately. We can't afford to wait, but we must remember that hope and the odds don't always align. More often than not, hope finds a way to triumph over overwhelming odds."

Commander Vela, ever the strategist, chimed in, "We also need to coordinate with other rebel cells. If we can synchronize our attacks, we'll have a much better chance of overwhelming Virox's defenses."

The team spent hours meticulously mapping out their strategy, examining every possible angle and contingency with painstaking care. They knew that any mistake, however small, could cost countless lives, but their determination never wavered. They were committed to seeing this through to the end, driven by a shared belief in the cause and the hope that their efforts would finally turn the tide of the war.

* * *

In the crew's quarters, Kael and Princess Quann shared a moment of quiet reflection, looking out at the frozen landscape of Glacius through a small viewport. The planet's surface glowed under the pale light of its distant sun, creating a serene but harsh beauty.

Kael spoke softly, his tone full of admiration, "You've shown incredible strength, Princess Quann. We couldn't have made it this far without you."

Princess Quann smiled, her eyes filled with hope's expectation of good, "And I couldn't have done it without all of you. This fight is far from over, but I know we can win."

Kael, his resolve unshaken, nodded, "We will. Together."

* * *

The following morning, the base was a hive of activity as preparations for the next phase of their mission began in earnest. The crew of the Starfire, now bolstered by the resources and support of the rebel base on Glacius, prepared for their next move against Virox. Engineers worked on the Starfire, ensuring it was in top condition for the upcoming battles. Weapons were checked and rechecked, and supplies were loaded onto ships.

Kael, Mara, Riz, and Princess Quann met with Vela and other key leaders in the base's command centre. The atmosphere was charged with a mix of anticipation and urgency.

Commander Vela addressed the group, "We've analised the data, and we're ready to move. Our primary target is Virox's main supply depot. Disabling it will disrupt his operations and give us a significant advantage."

Kael added, "Our intel shows that the supply depot is heavily guarded, but if we strike quickly and decisively, we can take it out before Virox has a chance to respond."

Princess Quann, now fully briefed and ready, spoke with confidence, "I've reached out to our allies in the Federation. I had to convince them now is the time to strike rather than pull back to safety. They're ready to provide support. I convinced them that we need to act now."

Riz, always the pragmatic one, chimed in, "Timing is everything. We need to synchronize our attack with the other rebel cells. If we hit multiple targets simultaneously, Virox's forces will be spread too thin to mount an effective defence."

Vela nodded, "Agreed. We've already started coordinating with other cells. Our attack will be the signal for them to strike."

As final preparations were made, the crew of the Starfire and the rebels of Glacius stood united in their resolve. They knew the road ahead was fraught with danger, but their willpower was unshaken.

* * *

The next day, the Starfire lifted off from Glacius, its engines roaring as it ascended through the planet's thick atmosphere. The crews were focused, each member of each team knowing their role in the upcoming mission. Kael piloted the ship with a steady hand, navigating the turbulent skies with practiced ease.

In the Starfire briefing room, the team gathered around a holographic display, reviewing the details of their plan one last time. The tension could be cut with a knife but so was the sense of purpose.

Mara addressed the group, "Remember, our primary objective is to disable the supply depot. Secondary objectives include gathering any intel we can find and causing as much disruption as possible."

Riz added, "We've loaded extra supplies and ammunition. We're ready for whatever comes our way."

Princess Quann, her eyes steely with determination, nodded, "We're doing this for everyone who has suffered under Virox's rule. Let's make it count."

Kael looked around the room, meeting the eyes of each of his crew members, "We've come this far together, and we'll see it through to the end. Let's go."

* * *

As the Starfire entered hyperspace, the crew settled into their routines, each person focusing on their tasks. The journey was tense but uneventful, and soon they emerged into normal space near their target.

The supply depot loomed ahead, a massive planetary structure bristling with defences. Kael guided the Starfire into position, and the crew prepared for the assault.

"Deploying cloaking device," Mara announced, as she slid her fingers over the controls, "We should be able to get close without being detected."

The cloaked ship vanished into the black emptiness of outer space. It moved in silent invisibility through the vacuous void. They approached the cluster of twelve ally ships of every size and shape that waited in silence for their arrival. Their hearts pounded with anticipation.

Kael's voice was calm and steady, "I'm serious, I say it over and over again; Remember, stick to the ideas we have talked about and we hit them hard and fast."

The Starfire closed in on the Virox supply depot, and the crew braced for the battle to come. As they prepared to strike, they knew that the future of the entire galaxy rested on the execution of their skills and ability to work as a team. If they took out Virox's supply depot the war against Virox would all but be over. United by a common goal and strengthened by their shared experiences, they were ready to face whatever challenges lay ahead.

The Starfire was the lead ship with eight other fighters close behind. The depot was fully fortified. Laser cannons in strategically placed turrets began to fire.

Captain Kael Ventara maneuvered the Starfire skillfully, dodging the first volley of enemy fire. The smaller fighters, nimble and quick, darted around the supply depot, drawing the turrets' fire and providing cover for the Starfire. Explosions lit up the dark expanse of space as the FAF ships returned fire, their lasers striking the supply depot's defenses.

"Shields holding at 80%," reported Mara Steeler, while she slid control bars on the glowing panel, "We need to take out those turrets or we won't last long."

"Riz, target the primary turret array," Kael ordered. "Mara, prepare for evasive maneuvers. Everyone, stay sharp."

Riz Talon, the ship's weapons expert, locked onto the main turret and fired a concentrated blast. The explosion was immediate and spectacular, sending debris flying. The FAF fighters took advantage of the momentary confusion, pressing their attack with renewed vigor.

Inside the supply depot, Virox's forces scrambled to mount a defense, but the coordinated assault by the FAF left them struggling. The Starfire's crew maintained relentless pressure, systematically obliterating the supply depot's defenses.

One by one, the turrets fell into smoldering silence.

"All turrets neutralized!" Riz announced triumphantly.

"Good work," Kael responded. "Now let's finish this."

With the supply depot's defenses crippled, the FAF ships closed in for the final assault. They targeted the main power generator, unleashing a barrage of laser fire. The generator erupted in a massive explosion, the shockwave rippling through the supply depot.

The Virox supply depot was left in a shamble of steel and concrete, its formidable structure now a ruin. Flames and smoke billowed into space, signaling the end of a significant threat. The FAF had won.

Cheers erupted within the Starfire. Kael looked at his crew, pride swelling in his chest. "We did it," he said. "With the supply depot destroyed the war against Virox is as good as over."

United by their victory and the expectation of success, they knew this was just the beginning of a new chapter for the galaxy. The supply depot lay in ruins, a testament to their bravery and determination. The future was theirs to shape.

With the battle over and little damage to the FAF ships the squadron silently returned to the icy planet of Glacius. Despite how cold the icy home base was it represented a safe refuge and a rallying point, where hope was put into action and plans were set in motion. Now, with hope turning to reality and the expectation of further success, with their resolve unshaken and their spirits high, they stood ready to strike back against tyranny. The battle for freedom continued, with the crew of the Starfire more determined than ever to see it through to the end.

Hope shines brightest when the world is at its dimmest.

Darkness amplifies the power of hope,
making it a beacon in times of despair.
When all else fades, hope emerges
with a clarity and brilliance that guides us
through the shadows.
It is in these moments that hope's light becomes
most essential,
showing us the way forward.

Chapter 15

Mission 'Hope Beyond Hope'

After a few days of rest and recuperation at the secret Freedom Alliance Fighters (FAF) base on the icy planet of Glacius, led by Rebel Leader Commander Vela, the crew of the Starfire received new orders. They were to rendezvous at a different FAF star base, led by Commander Peddler. This second resilient group, commanded by a seasoned fighter known only by his nickname, Peddler, had been waging a guerilla war against Virox's tyranny for years. Kael, Mara, Riz, and Princess Quann would join forces with all of the cells of the FAF and the Galactic Federation, uniting their strength for a coordinated assault on Virox's fleet.

* * *

The Starfire and numerous size and shapes of Commander Vela's ships sped through hyperspace, navigating towards the hidden base of Commander Peddler's FAF. The crew prepared for their meeting with the underground fighters, their minds focused on the battle ahead.

Kael, in the cockpit, kept his eyes on the swirling tunnel of hyperspace, "We're almost there. The FAF base is located in an asteroid field just beyond the Zandari Belt. Stay sharp."

Mara, checking her blaster, nodded, "I've heard about Peddler. They say he's a genius when it comes to guerilla warfare."

Riz, adjusting the ship's sensors, looked up, "He'll need to be if we're going to take down Virox's fleet."

Princess Quann, her gaze steady and determined, added, "With all of the cells of the FAF and the Federation united, we stand a chance. Let's make it count. At least now there is no supply depot to supply any of their ships. We just have to keep ducking out of sight while they run out of ammunition."

The Starfire emerged from hyperspace near the Kandari Belt. The asteroid field known by its nickname "The Rat's Maze" loomed ahead, a treacherous maze of rock and debris. Kael deftly piloted the ship through the field, following the coordinates provided by the FAF.

* * *

The hidden base of the FAF came into view, a series of camouflaged structures built into a large asteroid. The Starfire landed in a bustling hangar, surrounded by ships of various makes and models, all bearing the marks of countless battles.

Kael disembarked first, scanning the area, "Stay alert. We're among allies, but this place is a fortress for a reason."

A five foot, five inch, rugged man with a scarred face and piercing eyes approached them, flanked by heavily armed soldiers. His presence commanded respect and exuded experience.

Commander Peddler grinned, "Welcome to the heart of the rebellion. I'm Commander Peddler but just call me Peddler. You must be the infamous Captain Kael Ventara of the GFF. Your reputation precedes you."

Kael shook Commander Peddler's hand, "That's right. As you know we had a stopover for a few days with Commander Vela to lick our wounds and celebrate our success of rescuing Princess Quann, though it was not exactly a holiday considering we just took out the Virox supply depot. We're here to join forces and take the battle to the next step. The time has come to strike a crippling blow to Virox's fleet."

Commander Peddler nodded, "Follow me. We have much to discuss about the files that you sent me. What we have found on these files will add to our success a thousand fold." Reaching out to put his arm around the shoulder of Princess Quann, he thanked her, "I understand that we can all thank you for these amazing files. I think it is ironic to think that you gathered this intel because Virox captured you and took you into his laird."

* * *

Peddler took a jovial jab at Commander Vela, "You will find our headquarters a lot warmer than Vela's quaint little icy nook. Just to keep me humble she complains about how hot our headquarters are. We have to work with what we have. I can't offer you any ice for a glass of water the way Vela can but our water is just as wet. The group entered a large, strategic planning room within the FAF asteroid base. Holographic maps of Virox's fleet and key positions hovered above a round table. Leaders from the FAF, the Galactic Federation, and the Starfire crew gathered around, their faces grim but resolute.

Commander Peddler pointed to the map, "Virox's fleet is spread thin, but his command ship is heavily fortified. We need a coordinated attack to create a breach."

Kael studied the map on his comm-tablet, "We'll lead the assault on his flagship. If we can take out his command centre, it'll throw his forces into disarray."

Ambassador Zane, was already on Peddler's hidden base. He wanted to be in the thick of things for what he called the final battle. Other Federation ships were on their way waiting for orders. Zane's face, lined with worry, agreed, "Our ships will engage the main fleet, drawing their fire. Meanwhile, the FAF will disrupt their supply lines and communications. This should disrupt them so much that they won't know whether they are coming or going."

Princess Quann, her voice unwavering, added, "We must be swift and decisive. Virox will not hesitate to crush us if we falter."

Commander Peddler smirked, "He won't get the chance. We've been planning this for a long time. With this new intel it's time to execute."

The room fell silent as everyone absorbed the gravity of the situation. The plan was risky, but it was their best shot at dealing a significant blow to Virox's power.

Commander Peddler looked seriously at the group, "Let's call this mission 'Hope Beyond Hope'. We have been hoping and dreaming beyond hope for too long now. Let's hope it is finally here."

The group raised their fist in the air, "Hope Beyond Hope".

* * *

In the asteroid base's launch bay, the combined forces prepared for departure. Scout ships, fighters, bombers, and capital ships powered up, ready for the coming battle. The air was filled with the hum of engines and the clatter of weapons being checked and loaded.

Kael addressed his crew, "I know you get tired of me saying the same thing time and time again. But this is it. Remember your training, trust in each other, and we'll make it through. For the galaxy, and for freedom."

Mara was assigned her own fighter and crew. She and her team climbed in, her eyes blazing with strength of mind, "Is everyone strapped in? Let's show Virox what we're made of."

Riz prepped the Starfire's weapons, his hands moving swiftly over the panel, "I've tuned the Starfire's systems. She's ready for a fight."

Princess Quann strapped in, her voice calm and resolute, "May the Divine guide us."

* * *

Deep in space, near Virox's fleet, the combined forces of the FAF and the Galactic Federation emerged from hyperspace, immediately engaging in a massive space battle. The void erupted with laser fire and explosions as ships clashed in a deadly dance of warfare.

Commander Peddler's voice crackled over the comms, "All units, engage! Target their capital ships and protect the bombers!"

Kael piloted the Starfire with precision, weaving through enemy fire, "We're going for Chancellor Virox's flagship. Mara, cover our approach. Riz, keep those shields up."

Mara flew in formation, her ship darting through the chaos. With a smile she spoke over the comm-system, "I am on your port side, Kael. For this battle you are stuck with me as your wingman. Sorry about that. Let's do this."

The battle raged, with star fighters weaving through laser fire and capital ships exchanging devastating volleys. Explosions lit up the void as ships on both sides were hit. The combined forces fought valiantly, their resolve unwavering despite the overwhelming odds.

* * *

The impressive mass of Virox's flagship loomed ahead, a massive and intimidating structure. The Starfire along with Mara's fighter, amid heavy fire landed on the giant flagships hull. The shields on both ships flickering but holding. Kael and his team, Mara and hers disembarked, joining the assault teams making their way to entry ports.

Kael drew his lightsaber, its blue blade humming to life, "We need to reach the command centre. That's where Virox will be."

Mara, blasting at enemy soldiers, nodded, "We've got your back, Kael. Let's move!"

Riz covered their advance, his blaster firing in rapid succession, "Everyone, watch out for those drop down lasers hidden in the ceiling of just about every corridor! If you don't strike them first they will tear you apart!"

Princess Quann, fighting alongside them with fierce determination, rallied the troops, "Forward! We can't let them stop us now!"

As they breached the colossal entrance of Virox's flagship, the team plunged into the labyrinthine corridors, where Virox's elite troops awaited them at every turn. A relentless barrage of blaster fire erupted, sending sparks flying off the walls. The clash of energy blades and the crack of shields absorbing hits reverberated through the narrow passages, while the acrid scent of ozone filled the air. With each step forward, the team faced a new wave of enemies, their movements swift and coordinated, driven by the urgent need to reach their objective.

* * *

Kael led the charge, his lightsaber cutting through the enemy ranks, "This way! The command centre is just ahead!"

Commander Peddler joined the fight, his blaster blazing, "Keep pushing! Virox is within our grasp!"

Princess Quann, her voice strong and inspiring, rallied the troops, "We are fighting for freedom and justice! Don't let up! Hope beyond Hope."

The team reached the doors of the command centre, which were heavily fortified. Kael, Mara,

Riz, and Princess Quann took cover as Commander Peddler and his soldiers set up explosives to breach the entrance.

With a thunderous explosion, the doors blasted open. Kael and his team stormed in, confronting Virox and his personal guards.

Virox, standing calmly in the centre of the room, sneered, "Ventara. I expected you."

Kael stepped forward, his lightsaber at the ready, "This ends now, Virox."

Chancellor Virox drew his own lightsaber, its blade casting an ominous glow, "We shall see."

The room erupted into chaos as Kael once again engaged Virox in a fierce lightsaber duel, while Mara, Riz, and Princess Quann took on the guards. The clash of lightsabers and the roar of blasters filled the air.

Chancellor Virox taunted Kael as they fought, "You think you can defeat me? You're nothing but a child playing at war."

Kael, his fortitude unwavering, responded with a fierce strike, "We'll see who the child is."

* * *

The duel between Kael and Virox intensified, with both combatants showcasing their extraordinary skill. Sparks flew as their lightsabers clashed, each strike echoing through the command centre.

Kael, panting and pushing back against Virox's strikes, spoke through gritted teeth, "You won't win, Virox. The galaxy will never bow to you."

Virox, sneering, replied with a vicious attack, "Then it will burn."

With a final, desperate move, Kael disarmed Virox, sending his lightsaber clattering across the floor. But Virox was not finished yet. Knocking Kael back with a powerful thud he created a gap between them. Seizing the opportunity, Virox leaped to a lower platform, escaping into a lower level of corridors, expecting to lead Kael into a disadvantaged location.

Kael shouted into the void, "There you go again taking the cowards way out. Just like the last time we locked sabers. As soon as you are close to being defeated you run like a baby spider rat looking for his mommy."

Kael, breathing heavily, called out to his team, "He's getting away! We need to finish this!"

Mara helped Kael to his feet, her eyes filled with concern, "We will but first, let's secure the ship."

* * *

The aftermath of the battle saw the combined forces of the FAF and the Galactic Federation securing Virox's flagship, capturing his remaining troops and taking control of the ship. The victory was hard-fought, but it marked yet another significant turning point in their struggle against Virox.

Commander Peddler rallied the fighters, his voice echoing through the halls, "We've done it! Virox's fleet is in disarray. Now is the time to press our advantage!"

Princess Quann addressed the troops, her voice carrying a message of hope and determination, "Today, we have struck a mighty blow against tyranny. But the fight is not over. We must continue to stand united until Virox is truly defeated."

Kael, standing with his friends, looked out over the gathered forces, "We've made great strides today, but we must remain vigilant. The final battle is still ahead. Total victory is not ours until Virox has been slain."

*Hope is the ever-present flower
of opportunity.*

*Life's prospects change,
bringing both abundance and scarcity,
yet hope remains in perpetual bloom.
It is the perennial flower
that adds colour and fragrance to life,
enduring through every season,
unaffected by the external conditions
that would wither possibilities with fear.*

Chapter 16

One more Battle to be Fought

Virox's forces are crumbling. With the supply depot crippled and in smoke and Virox's flagship captured, the tide has turned in favor of the forces of good. The united strength of the FAF and the GFF have dealt a significant blow to Virox's power. As they regrouped and prepared for the final confrontation, hope burned brighter than ever. The battle for the galaxy's freedom continued, with Kael, Mara, Riz, Princess Quann, and their new allies Commander Peddler and Commander Vela leading the charge.

The stage was set for the ultimate showdown, where the fate of the galaxy would be decided once and for all. United by their common goal and strengthened by their shared experiences, the forces of good stood ready to face the challenges ahead. The final battle loomed on the horizon, promising to be the most intense and decisive conflict yet.

As the crew of the Starfire prepared for what lay ahead, they knew that their journey was far from over. The road to victory would be long and demanding, but their resolve was unshaken. Together, they would fight for the freedom of the galaxy, standing inspiration of hope against the darkness that threatened to consume them all.

* * *

The crew's quarters aboard the Starfire were quiet as they reflected on the day's events. Kael and Princess Quann stood by the viewport, gazing out at the vast expanse of space.

Kael broke the silence, his voice filled with determination, "We've come a long way, Quann but the hardest part of hunting down Chancellor Virox for the final battle is still ahead. We can't afford to let him slip into safety and rebuild his empire. He will have already hidden away in a safe place."

Princess Quann nodded, her expression resolute, "I know, Kael. But we have something Virox will never understand: hope. As long as we have that, we can never be truly defeated."

Kael smiled, drawing strength from her words, "You're right. And with the FAF, the Federation, and everyone willing to fight by our side, we will prevail."

* * *

The following morning, the base was abuzz with activity as preparations for the final assault began in earnest. The captured flagship was being retrofitted and repaired, its systems integrated with the combined fleet's operations. Computer engineers worked tirelessly unscrambling encrypted files hoping to gain more information that could guide the FAF into a greater advantage. Engineers worked tirelessly, ensuring that everything was in top condition for the upcoming battle.

Kael, Mara, Riz, and Princess Quann met with Commander Peddler and the other leaders in the base's command centre. The air was charged with urgency, but also with comradeship and respect.

Commander Peddler addressed the group, his voice steady and confident, "Chancellor Virox has escaped to one of his other ships. Which one we don't know but we will find him."

Kael interrupted, "We will take care of Virox later but for now, our new intel shows that the headquarters is weakening. We will have to strike quickly while we have the advantage. We are in a perfect position to take it out before Virox has a chance to respond."

Princess Quann, now fully briefed and ready, spoke, "I've just talked to Ambassador Zane. He said he is ready to provide tactical support, but we need to act now."

* * *

Restlessness pervaded the Starfire's corridors the night before the mission. Every team member, from the seasoned veterans to the newest recruits, felt the significance of the impending battle. No one wanted to voice the reality that tomorrow's confrontation would be a make-or-break moment, one that would echo through history.

The following day, the Starfire ascended from the asteroid base, its engines thundering into the silent vacuum of space. The crew was focused. Not a single joke or kibitzing came from any of the teams as they readied for the mission. Each member was acutely aware of their crucial role in the name of success. Kael piloted the Starfire with the calm of a seasoned pro navigating in slow motion from the ice lined docking bay.

Once the ship was slipped into auto pilot the team assembled around a holographic display gazing at hope beyond hope, tweaking plans one last time.

Mara addressed the group, "I have said it many times in the last couple of days but I will say it one more time, our primary objective is to disable the Virox headquarters the way we did the supply depot. We have to do this in any way possible. Don't be distracted by anything else." Mara paused for a moment, "But keep in mind our secondary objectives are to gather any intel and cause as much disruption to the Virox fleet as possible."

Riz stepped forward, "As you know we have stocked extra ammunition on all of the ships. With this extra armament our objective is to do as much damage as possible. If we can leave nothing but charred steel and smoke we will have done our job."

Princess Quann stood silently, as if whispering to a guiding angel, "At this point we are beyond hope. We have to stand strong and know, know that there is only one outcome and that outcome is victory. We have come a long way. There is no turning back. We are moving from hope, to knowing, to victory. We must embrace the expectation of success, believing with every fiber of our being that triumph is inevitable."

Kael looked around the room, meeting the eyes of each of his crew members, noting everyone's victorious resolve, "I am proud of everything that we have done. As Mara has said we have looked death in the face and survived but we are going to have to do it one more time. We've come this far and we will see it through to the end. Let's take it one more rung up the ladder of success."

With a great sense of determination Kael pushed the throttle arm forward. The Starfire jumped into hyperspace, the crew settled into their routines, focusing on their tasks. The journey was emotionally calm and uneventful. They soon emerged from hyperspace near their target.

The lead ship loomed ahead, a massive structure bristling with defences. Kael guided the Starfire into position as the crew prepared for the assault.

"All is ready on this end," Mara announced with confidence, "We should be able to get close without being detected."

The ship shimmered and vanished from the enemy's sensors, moving silently through the void. They approached the headquarters, hearts pounding.

Kael's voice was calm, "Don't forget my mantra; Remember, stick to the plan. We hit them hard and fast."

The Starfire, supported by Commander Peddler's ship, closed in on the headquarters. The crew braced for the battle to come. They knew that the fate of the galaxy rested on their shoulders. United by a common goal and strengthened by their shared experiences, they were ready to face whatever challenges lay ahead.

As the cloaked Starfire edged closer to the headquarters, tension increased. Mara monitored the sensors, ensuring they remained undetected. Riz and his team double-checked their weapons and equipment, ready for the imminent conflict. Princess Quann mentally prepared herself for the task ahead.

"Approaching target," Kael announced, his voice under control despite the rising pressure.

The Starfire halted just outside of the lead ships sensor range. Mara deactivated the cloaking device, and the ship reappeared, now in striking distance.

"All teams, prepare for deployment," Kael ordered.

The crew moved with synchronized precision, boarding their assault craft and readying themselves for the infiltration. Kael remained on the bridge, coordinating the attack and monitoring enemy movements.

As the assault teams launched from the Starfire, Commander Peddler's ship provided covering fire, drawing the depot's defences away from the infiltration units. Explosions rocked the lead ship as the enemy scrambled to respond to the sudden attack.

"Team Alpha, move to disable the primary power generators," Mara's voice crackled over the comms, "Team Beta, secure the command centre."

The infiltration teams moved swiftly, using the element of surprise to their advantage. Blaster fire echoed through the corridors of the lead ship as the teams engaged enemy forces. Riz led Team Alpha, cutting through enemy lines with precision and efficiency. Mara, heading Team Beta, navigated the convoluted passages toward the command centre.

Princess Quann and her elite squad targeted the battery, planting explosives to maximize the disruption. Exploding their armaments would do plenty of damage. With each step, they moved closer to their objective: they would make every second count.

"Generators disabled," Riz reported, his voice filled with earnestness.

"Command centre secure," Mara confirmed, her team already accessing the ship's data banks.

"Explosives set," Princess Quann announced, "We're ready for extraction."

Kael coordinated the attach, guiding the assault teams back to the Starfire. As the last team boarded, he initiated the retreat sequence. The headquarters, now crippled and on the brink of total destruction, was left behind as the Starfire and Commander Peddler's ship jumped back into hyperspace.

The mission was a success, but the crew knew the war was far from over. Once again, they had struck a substantial blow against Virox's forces. Despite the success of the mission no one dare think about the many battles that still lay ahead. United by their shared resolve and the knowledge that they were fighting for a just cause, the crew of the Starfire prepared for the next challenge. Together, they would continue their fight for freedom, intent on finding Virox and bringing an end to his tyranny.

Hope is the invisible thread that pulls us through our darkest days.

When life seems to unravel before our very eyes,
hope is the unseen force
that keeps us from being swallowed by fear.
Like a delicate thread,
it weaves through our dread,
pulling us
toward the light of progress and growth.

Chapter 17

The Infiltration of the Dominator

The Dominator, the second largest ship in the Virox fleet, second only to the newly captured Virox lead flag ship, loomed ahead, an imposing silhouette against the stars. It was mammoth. This colossal vessel overflowed with weaponry and was a symbol of Chancellor Virox's tyranny. Among its many more traditional laser weapons it featured what was nicknamed the "superlaser" that could fire faster and further with more anticipatory precision than had ever been engineered. To make things worse, it could fire at eight targets at a time. Compared to smaller, more agile starships, it lugged along like a Blue Whale being chased by a Shortfin Mako Shark. The Dominator was known more for its invincibility rather than its speed and agility. It was an intimidating sight, but for Kael Ventara and Princess Quann, it represented their next challenge in the fight for freedom. They approached the behemoth in a stolen shuttle, disguised as maintenance workers, their faces set in grim strength of character.

Kael adjusted his disguise, his voice steady but laced with urgency, "We're almost there. Remember, act natural. We need to blend in until we reach the main weapon control centre."

Princess Quann, nervously fiddling with her tools, nodded, "Got it. I just hope our intel is accurate."

Kael gave her a reassuring glance, "It will be. We've come this far. We can do this."

As they entered the hangar bay, the scale of their task became evident. The bay was in full activity—workers, droids, and guards all moving. Kael and Quann disembarked from their shuttle, blending into the throng with ease. They made their way towards a maintenance elevator, carefully avoiding the watchful eyes of the guards.

A guard, eyeing them suspiciously, called out, "Hey, you two! What's your business here?"

Kael quickly showed their forged identification, "Maintenance crew. We've got orders to check the primary coolant systems."

The guard, still wary, grudgingly allowed them to pass, "Alright, but make it quick. We're on high alert."

As they entered the elevator, Quann let out a breath she hadn't realized she was holding, "That was close."

Kael whispered back, "Stay focused. We're just getting started."

The elevator descended into the bowels of the ship, the atmosphere growing more oppressive with each passing moment. The flickering lights and distant hum of machinery added to the tension. Kael and Quann prepared for the next step.

Kael checked his equipment, "Once we're out, we head straight for the main weapon control. No detours."

Quann nodded, her strength of will matching his, "Understood. Let's disable that superlaser and end this nightmare."

The elevator doors opened to a dimly lit corridor. They moved swiftly but cautiously, avoiding patrols and security cameras. The closer they got to the main weapon control centre, the tighter the security became. Heavily armed guards and multiple security checkpoints stood between them and their goal.

Kael and Quann hid behind a bulkhead, formulating their plan. Kael whispered, "We need a distraction. If we can draw some of the guards away, we'll have a better chance."

Princess Quann, thinking quickly, pointed to a power conduit nearby, "I have an idea. There's a power conduit over there. If we overload it, it should create a distraction big enough."

Kael smiled at her ingenuity, "Good thinking. Let's do it."

Quann carefully rigged the conduit to overload. Sparks flew, and smoke began to billow out, triggering alarms throughout the area. Guards rushed to contain the apparent malfunction.

One of the guards shouted, "Fire in section 12! Get the extinguishers!"

Kael motioned to Quann, "Now's our chance. Go!"

They slipped past the distracted guards and made their way into the main weapon control centre. The room was filled with advanced technology and displays monitoring the superlaser. Kael quickly accessed the control panel while Quann kept watch, her blaster at the ready.

Kael's fingers glided over the smooth dimly lit control panel as if they had a mind of their own, "I'm in. Cover me while I disable the weapon. I need to rip out a few of these modulators and I am done."

Quann scanning the room for any threats, urged Kael on, "Hurry, Kael. We are already two minutes past our estimated time."

As Kael worked on disabling the weapon, a voice echoed through the room. They turned to see a hologram of Chancellor Virox materializing in the centre, his face twisted in a cruel smile.

Virox smirked, "Ah, Kael Ventara and Princess Quann. Did you really think it would be this easy?"

Kael's anger flared, "Virox! Where are you?"

Virox mockingly replied, "Safe and sound, far away from here. But I must commend your bravery. It's actually admirable."

The walls of the chamber flashed with the image of Virox, his presence menacing. Quann stepped forward; her voice defiant, "You can't hide forever, Virox. We will find you, and not just stop you but crush you."

Virox laughed, a cold and hollow sound, "Such fire. But it's misplaced. My forces are vast, and my plans are already in motion. You are too late."

Kael finished his work on the control panel, shutting down the superlaser, "We'll see about that. Princess Quann, let's go!"

Virox's hologram sputtered ominously, "Run while you can, Ventara. This is far from over."

With the main weapon disabled, Kael and Quann made their escape. Alarms blared. Guards closed in from all directions. They fought their way through the corridors, taking out guards and avoiding security traps. Their closeness was reinforced as they relied on each other for survival.

Kael, breathing heavily, led the way, "This way! The hangar bay is just ahead."

Quann, firing at approaching guards, stayed close, "I've got your back. Keep moving!"

They reached the hangar bay, where their stolen shuttle awaited. Dodging blaster fire, they sprinted towards it. Kael shouted, "Get in! I'll cover you!"

Quann climbed aboard, urging Kael to hurry, "OK Kael, come on. I am in, let's go!"

Kael leaped into the shuttle, sealing the hatch behind him. They lifted off, escaping the Dominator as it erupted into chaos.

In the vast expanse of space just outside the Dominator, the shuttle sped away. Kael set the course, his relief palpable, "We did it. The superlaser is offline."

Quann, equally relieved but focused on the larger battle ahead, responded, "But Virox is still out there. We need to regroup with the others and plan our next move."

Kael nodded, his resolve ablaze, "We will. Together."

Hope is the bridge that carries us over
the river of despair.

Despair can feel like an insurmountable barrier,
but hope builds bridges
where none existed before.
It connects us to the other side,
offering a way across the turbulent waters
of doubt and fear.
With hope, no gap is too wide,
no obstacle too great.

Chapter 18

The Final Confrontation

The central command chamber of Virox's Headquarters was a dimly lit and imposing room filled with advanced technology and holographic displays. The oppressive room spelled tension as Kael, Riz, Mara, and Princess Quann entered, their weapons ready. This was the moment they had been preparing for. It was bound to be the final confrontation that would determine the fate of the galaxy.

Virox stood at the far end of the room, smiling cruelly as he was flanked by his elite guards, "Ah, Captain Kael Ventara and his ragtag band of rebels. You're just in time for the grand finale.

What took you so long. I have been patiently waiting here for you. I was starting to get bored."

Kael stepped forward, his lightsaber ignited, its blue glow illuminating his face, "This ends now, Virox. Your reign of terror is over."

Virox laughed, a cold, mirthless sound, "Such bravado. But you've always been predictable, Kael. Let's see if you can back up your words with action."

The room erupted into chaos as Virox's guards attacked. Kael, Riz, Mara, and Princess Quann engaged in fierce combat, their movements unstoppable as they fought for their lives and the future of the galaxy.

Mara, taking down a guard with a swift move, shouted, "Keep pushing! We can't let them overwhelm us!"

Riz fired his blaster, covering Mara's back, "Watch out, Mara! There are more coming!"

Princess Quann fought with grace and fortitude, her movements a wave of precision, "We've come too far to fail now. Sovereignty and independence are the only choices.!"

Amidst the chaos of the battles raging across the ship, the clash between Kael and Virox took center stage. The air crackled with the energy of their duel, each strike of their lightsabers sending showers of sparks cascading through the dimly lit chamber. The room seemed to pulse with the intensity of their conflict, every clash reverberating through the walls.

Virox's face twisted into a sneer, his eyes glinting with a cruel satisfaction. His attacks were relentless and precise, a deadly dance of aggression. "Still playing soldier boy, Kael? You're nothing more than a child in over his head. This war is beyond you." Kael, unfazed, responds with a similarly repetitive retort, "You haven't learned, Virox. We're not backing down. This time, we finish what we started."

Kael's teeth were clenched as he met each of Virox's blows with fierce determination, his muscles straining under the weight of the dark energy surrounding them. His movements were a blur of calculated precision, his lightsaber a beacon of hope amidst the oppressive darkness that sought to engulf him. Every swing, every parry, was infused with the fire of his unyielding resolve.

"You underestimate me, Virox, because you have no idea of the power of hope." Kael retorted, his voice steady and clear, cutting through the cacophony of their clashing blades. "Hope is not just a fleeting emotion or a wish upon the stars. It's a force more real and more potent than the energy that fuels your hatred and greed."

He pressed forward, his strikes becoming more aggressive, forcing Virox back. "I'm not fighting alone," Kael continued, his voice rising with the crescendo of the battle. "What you don't understand is that I have the greatest ally. An ally you could never comprehend, let alone possess. The ally of hope and the expectancy of good."

Kael's eyes burned with intensity as he locked gazes with his adversary. "Fear blocks the possibility to hope, and you, Virox, are the very embodiment of fear. You're so consumed by it that you can't see past your need for power, past the darkness that blinds you to the truth."

He advanced again, each step forward a testament to his unbreakable spirit. "But hope is different. It doesn't bow to fear. It thrives in the face of it, it grows stronger in the shadows. And that's why you'll never win, Virox. Because all your fear will let you see is your insatiable hunger for power, while I see the light beyond the darkness. I see hope and the inevitability of good."

Virox's laugh was a harsh, mocking sound as he leaned on his lightsaber with an air of condescension, as if it were a theatrical cane. "Let's see just how far your so-called expectancy of good will get you," he jeered. "Let's see if it will get you any further than your poor training and skill."

The battle continued to rage, a deadly ballet of skill and willpower. Kael drew upon his inner strength and the unwavering support of his friends, each memory of their sacrifices fueling his resolve. Virox's taunts were like a twisted symphony, pushing Kael to dig deeper into his reserves of courage. With each passing moment, Kael's movements grew more fluid, his strikes more powerful and accurate, as if the weight of his understanding of hope was guiding his blade.

Kael's voice rang out with a fierce, unwavering conviction as he parried a particularly brutal assault. "This is for everyone you've hurt, Virox," he proclaimed, echoing Princess Quann's whispered encouragement just before they entered the fray. "For all the lives you've destroyed."

Virox's smirk did not waver, his posture relaxed even as he continued his assault. "You think you can defeat me?" he sneered, the arrogance in his voice palpable. "I've been training for over a century. You're nothing but a little weakling."

Kael's grip tightened around his lightsaber, a steely resolve burning in his eyes. Drawing upon every ounce of his strength, he executed a powerful, decisive strike that forced Virox's lightsaber from his hand. The weapon skidded across the floor, clattering to a halt several meters away. Virox staggered, his expression shifting from confidence to shock as he fell to his knees, blood trickling from his mouth.

Virox's gaze was one of stunned disbelief as he coughed, his voice a rasping whisper. "Impossible! How could I be defeated by you?"

Kael stood over him, his posture a testament to his triumph and resolve. His lightsaber gleamed with the reflection of his determination. "Because you fought only for yourself," Kael said, his voice ringing with authority. "Not for good, but only for you and your giant ego. The expectancy of good is not for me or any single person. It is for all humankind. It overcomes hope beyond hope. We all fought for something greater than the royal me."

Virox's eyes were wide with disbelief, a look of final, uncomprehending shock etched into his features as he collapsed, his body falling heavily to the floor. His last words were barely a whisper, a fading echo of his arrogance. "This... cannot be..."

The chamber fell into a profound silence, the echoes of their battle slowly fading into the distant hum of the ship's machinery. Kael stood victorious, his heart heavy with the weight of their struggle and the price of their victory. As he looked down at Virox's fallen form, he felt the gravity of the moment, knowing that the fight had not been just for him but for everyone who had suffered under Virox's tyranny. The path to peace and rebuilding lay ahead, and with the defeat of Virox, a new chapter began, marked by the strength of their unity and the power of their hope.

The room fell silent as Virox's lifeless body hit the ground. All fighting stopped as all of Virox's soldiers fled for personal safety. Kael stood over the grey body of Virox, breathing heavily, the solemnity of the moment settling in. Riz, Mara, and Princess Quann joined him, their faces reflecting a mix of liberation, triumph, freedom, emancipation, all of these dancing in their minds.

Riz clapped Kael on the back, "You did it, Kael. Virox is finally gone."

Mara smiled, wiping sweat from her brow, "We did it. Together."

Princess Quann embraced Kael, "The galaxy is free, thanks to you. Thanks to everyone that fought on the side of hope. We did it one impossible mission at a time."

* * *

In the aftermath of the battle, the combined forces of good secured Virox's Headquarters. Virox's soldiers who did not flee gave no resistance. A few guards were found cowering in dark corners hoping to be overlooked. The victors settled in to dismantle the Virox war room and take total control over technology, weapons and intel. The galaxy began to feel the first signs of freedom and hope.

Kael addressed the gathered allies and soldiers, "Today, we've shown that no tyrant can stand against the united will of the people. Virox's reign of terror is over, but our work is not done. We must rebuild, heal, and ensure that such darkness never returns."

Princess Quann stepped forward, her voice strong and clear, "Together, we will create a new era of peace and justice. The sacrifices we've made will not be in vain."

* * *

As the remnants of Virox's empire crumbled, Kael, Riz, Mara, and Quann stood together, reflecting on their journey. The central command chamber, now an icon of their victory, had been the setting for their final confrontation with the tyrant who had brought so much suffering to the galaxy.

Kael's mind wandered back to the beginning of their struggle. He remembered the first time he had met Princess Quann, the uncertainty they had faced, and the friends they had lost along the way. Now, standing in the heart of Virox's former bastion, he felt a sense of closure.

The aftermath of the battle was a whirlwind of activity. The allied forces worked tirelessly to secure the area, ensuring that no remnants of Virox's regime could regroup and pose a threat. The command centre, once a hub of Virox's power, was dismantled piece by piece.

Kael and his companions walked through the corridors, Their victory felt real. They passed by the cells where prisoners had been held, the control rooms where Virox had orchestrated his plans, and the armories that had supplied his forces. Each step they took was a step towards a brighter future.

Riz, ever the pragmatist, voiced his thoughts, "We've won a great battle today, but the war isn't over. There are still pockets of resistance, and Virox's followers won't give up easily."

Mara nodded, her eyes scanning their surroundings, "We need to stay vigilant. The galaxy is fragile right now, and it's up to us to protect the peace we've fought so hard to achieve."

Princess Quann's gaze was distant, her thoughts on the countless lives affected by Virox's tyranny, "We have a responsibility to those who suffered under Virox's rule. We must help them rebuild, give them hope, and ensure that such darkness never takes hold again."

Kael placed a hand on her shoulder, offering comfort, "We'll do it together. The four of us, and everyone who believes in a free galaxy. We've shown what we're capable of when we stand united."

**Hope in your heart,
will lead to great journeys.**

*Hope empowers action, no matter how small.
Each step, taken with hope,
becomes a part of a grander journey.
It reminds us that progress isn't always swift
or visible but it is inevitable.
With hope as our guide, even the smallest efforts
lead to meaningful change.*

Chapter 19

A Commitment to Rebuilding

The days that followed were devoted to rebuilding and recovery. Allied forces spread across the galaxy, liberating planets still under the shadow of Virox's influence. Humanitarian efforts were launched to aid those in need, and new alliances were formed to strengthen the ties between different star systems.

Kael, Riz, Mara, and Princess Quann became symbols of hope and resilience. Their story was told and retold, inspiring others to join the cause and fight for a better future. They travelled from planet to planet, meeting with leaders, rallying support, and overseeing reconstruction efforts.

On one particularly memorable day, they visited the planet of Eldoria, a once-thriving world that had been devastated by Virox's forces. The scars of war were still visible, but the spirit of the people was intact. Kael and his companions were greeted as heroes. Finally every member of the planet could take a rest. A rest from fighting, a rest from hopelessness, a rest from fear. Rebuilding would be a long slow process but first they will rest and mourn the people they lost. The joy of liberation was smothered by the sadness they carried. A sad day of remembrance was declared as an international holiday for ever to be know as "Hope against Hope". The entire planet wept in victory for all of the soles that had been lost.

* * *

In Princess Quann's capital city, they stood before a crowd of thousands, their faces lit in happiness. Kael addressed them, his voice carrying the optimistic message of their collective journey.

With a sense of pride beaming from his face, Kale spoke to the crowd, "People of Lumina, today we stand together as a testament to the strength and resilience of the Galactic Federation. We have faced great darkness, but we have emerged stronger and more united. The road to recovery will be long, but together we will rebuild and create a future where peace and justice prevail."

The crowd erupted in cheers, their voices echoing through the city. Kael looked at his companions, each of them sharing in the moment of triumph. Riz's eyes shone with pride, Mara's smile was radiant, and Princess Quann's gaze conveyed a quiet strength.

As the days turned into weeks and the weeks into months, the galaxy began to heal. Virox's name became a distant memory, a cautionary tale of tyranny and the power of the people to overcome it. Kael, Riz, Mara, and Quann continued their work, never losing sight of the goal they had fought so hard to achieve.

In a serene moment, Kael and Quann found themselves alone, overlooking a peaceful valley on a distant planet. The sun was setting, casting a warm glow over the landscape. They stood in silence, each lost in their thoughts.

Kael broke the silence, his voice soft, "We've come a long way, haven't we?"

Quann nodded, her eyes shimmering in the sunset. She spoke softly, "We have. And there's still so much to do. But I believe in us. I believe in what we can achieve together. Like you i believe in Hope. What was it that you told me that your grandfather used to say? Hope is never lost. There are always possibilities. Lack of hope simply means lack of faith and lack of imagination."

Kael took her hand, their fingers intertwined, "Yes that is it. And no matter what challenges we face, we will always have the faith and the imagination to keep going."

They stood there, side by side, watching the sun set on a galaxy that was beginning to find its light once more. The journey had been long and arduous, but they had emerged stronger, united by a common purpose and an indestructible link.

As the stars began to appear in the night sky, Kael and Quann knew that their story was far from over. They had won a great victory, but the fight for peace and justice would continue. And they would be there, leading the charge, ready to face whatever the future held.

For the galaxy, for their friends, and for each other, they would keep fighting. Because they knew that as long as they stood together, there was nothing they couldn't overcome.

The final confrontation with Virox had been a turning point, but it was just the beginning of a new chapter in their journey. As they looked towards the horizon, they knew that the best was yet to come.

*Hope is the gentle breeze
that lifts us when the fight is over.*

*When the battles of life are over,
hope governs, guides and guards us with its
gentle encouragement
to take the next step in the right direction.
Hope is a quiet support
that carries us forward in subtle ways
when we think we no longer have the strength.*

Epilogue

The Eternal Flame of Hope

As the galaxy settled into a newfound peace, the tale of Princess Quann and her brave rescuers became legend. The Ventara Adventures were repeated time and time again from one star systems to another. Stories were told far beyond the Galactic Federation. Their story a testament to the resilience of hope in the face of tyranny.

Chancellor Virox's reign of terror that lasted over many decades had been formidable, but the spirit of hope and the expectation of good had proved even stronger. The galaxy now flourished with freedom and justice, an example of what could be achieved when hope wasn't abandoned. Princess

Quann, once a captive, turned into a light showing her indomitable spirit, her courage inspiring countless others to stand up against oppression.

The Ventara team—Kael, Riz, and Mara—were celebrated as idols. They became ambassadors of hope working with the Galactic Federation rebuilding communities and entire planets. Their skills and ability to adapt had been tested to their limits. Beyond their bravery and skill, it was their continued hope that had carried them through the blackest moments.

From time to time Kael returned to the planet of Elyria to visit Master Elion were he continued to grow in his understanding and trust in the Divine.

Outside of the Grand Halls of the Galactic Federation's capital, a monument was erected to honour all of the heroes of *The Ventara Adventures*. At its centre burned an eternal flame, representing the hope that had driven them to victory. Inscribed upon the base of the monument were the words of Princess Quann: "Hope is the flame that guides us through the darkness. It is the light that reveals the path to freedom and justice. As long as we hold onto hope, no force can extinguish our spirit."

Afterword by the Editor,
Miguel Ángel Olivé Iglesias

Thus we come to the end of *The Ventara Adventures*—the end of this first part in the saga: the author is working on a sequel. I feel I must contribute a few Afterword lines with comments on the author´s philosophical standpoint. Müller´s adherence to hope and resilience, to improvement and a better future, is more than noticeable in the novel.

Hope for him is not just a passive wish for a better future. It is an active force, a driving energy that moves individuals into action, even when the odds are overwhelmingly against them. This kind of hope, according to Hans Müller—and I second this notion, is resilient because it is deeply rooted in the belief that change is possible, that no matter how dire the circumstances, there is always a path to a better outcome.

Resilience can be linked to the thought that hope is a response to the inherent uncertainties and absurdities of life. It is a leap of faith, an embrace of the unknown with the conviction that meaning and purpose can be found.

Throughout their journey, the Ventara team demonstrated how hope is also a shared force. It thrives in the collective dreams and aspirations of societies. The rescue of Princess Quann was not just the mission of a few brave souls but a resounding cry that united the galaxy in a common cause.

The spirit of hope lies in its dynamic nature too. It is not a static state but a continuous process of rebirth and adaptation. It invites individuals to embrace vulnerability, to find strength in their weaknesses, and to persist despite obstacles.

The resilience of hope is therefore interwoven with the expectation of good. Princess Quann and the entire Ventara team have hope blended with a steadfast belief in positive outcomes. Despite facing seemingly insurmountable challenges and dangers, their combined hope and faith in goodness prop their determination. This powerful synergy of positive expectation not only drives them forward but also strengthens their resolve to confront and overcome difficulties. In their quest for justice and freedom, this enduring hope and belief in the good become their guiding light and source of strength.

As I said in my Introduction, across the novel's pages we have now taken delight in the words of the romantic writer, the hopeful, optimistic author, who leaves for us lines of sheer tenderness and expectation; lines that reinforce the notions of determination and hope:

> "In a serene moment, Kael and Quann found themselves alone, overlooking a peaceful valley on a distant planet. The sun was setting, casting a warm glow over the landscape. They stood in silence, each lost in their thoughts. (…) They stood there, side by side, watching the sun set on a galaxy that was beginning to find its light once more. The journey had been long and arduous, but they had emerged stronger, united by a common purpose and an indestructible link. (…) The final confrontation with Virox had been a turning point, but it was just the beginning of a new chapter in their journey. And as they looked towards the horizon, they knew that the best was yet to come."

There is more than beauty in those lines; there is reassurance, survival spirit, faith, a constant flame of rebelliousness against injustice, optimism yet alertness for what might happen next. These virtues are valid in any context. I am certain readers will embark on these adventures, which take a quantum leap beyond rescue and fighting episodes in the novel to emerge as symbols of the hope and resilience the human race needs to move ever on.

Miguel Ángel Olivé Iglesias

Author Bio:

Born and raised in Berlin, Germany, 1960, Hans David Müller moved to a small town in Northern Ontario in 1982. With his unwavering supportive wife Christina, they raised three children; two boys and a girl, raised two goats, a dog, two cats and a pet pig they eventually ate because it got too big.

He taught his children the value of the resilience of hope and the expectancy of good, and to apply those essential life skills to everything they did. He has always had a strong affinity to his roots and his rich cultural history but with his love for forests, lakes and nature, Canada quickly became his new and beloved home.

He pursued a career in education, becoming a cherished and respected high school teacher, where he taught literature and history for almost four decades. His passion for teaching and storytelling was evident in his dynamic and engaging classes, inspiring countless students to explore their own creativity and curiosity. Upon retiring, Hans finally had the time to indulge in his lifelong dream of writing a novel. Drawing on his extensive knowledge of literature and his fondness for science fiction, in particular the "Star Wars" sagas and the little known sci-fi series called "Halo," his imaginative spirit drew him to write his debut novel, *The Ventara Adventures: The Resilience of Hope.* His passion for the characters in this first novel have developed into a second book entitled: *The Ventara Adventures – All for One and One for All.* His dream is that this might turn into a series.

Photograph by
Christina Müller

A short bio note about the Editor, Professor Miguel Ángel Olivé Iglesias. MSc

- Professor, University of Holguin, Cuba
- VP of the Canada Caribbean Literary Alliance
- Guest Member of the Mexican Association of Language and Lit Professors
- Author, Poet, Writer, Editor, Proofreader, Lit Reviewer, Translator
- CanLit Scholar

Dear Reader,

As Editor-in-Chief and publisher, I don't usually write an afterword, but I had such a great time reading and guiding this YA tale of capture and rescue that I couldn't resist the opportunity to share my thoughts. *The Ventara Adventures: The Resilience of Hope* offers a thrilling journey where good triumphs over evil, hope shines through despair, and heroism is tested in the face of danger. I would like to extend my heartfelt thanks to Hans David Müller for creating this engaging and inspiring debut novel.

Although I am a few years older than Hans, we share a common bond through the cultural icons that shaped our imaginations. Characters like Luke Skywalker, Princess Leia Organa, Captain James T. Kirk, and Spock left a lasting mark on both of us. Their adventures, courage, and determination influenced the way we saw the world and helped us navigate our own paths in life. These stories of heroism and perseverance resonate with me to this day.

Now, at the age of 70, I still find joy in revisiting these beloved characters. Watching reruns of "Star Wars" and "Star Trek" brings a sense of nostalgia and wonder that never fades. It's clear that Hans has drawn from the same well of inspiration, weaving his own story of bravery, friendship, and the triumph of hope over adversity. I hope you enjoyed reading this novel as much as I did, and that it brings you the same sense of adventure and inspiration.

I have had a glimpse at Hans' second novel, The *Ventara Adventures - All for One and One for All*. If you enjoyed this novel you will enjoy the second novel even more. Stay tuned for even greater adventures.

Sincerely,
Richard Marvin Tiberius Grove

Printed in the USA
CPSIA information can be obtained
at www.ICGtesting.com
JSHW030431081224
74995JS00006B/167